SYNOPSIS

You found parts of me I didn't know existed, and in you, I found a
love I no longer believed was real.
-Unknown

Shayna King is struggling to be happy again after tragically losing her
fiancé to murder and her parents to a drunk driver. The middle King
sister is now quiet and conservative, hiding the person she used to be.

Handsome photographer, Greg Navarro, looks like he should be
on the opposite end of the camera. His business is flourishing, and life
is good when he's introduced to the simple beauty that is Shayna
King.

Greg goes after what he wants, and he finds himself wanting
Shayna. Shayna is thrown off balance as an unspoken romance begins
between the two of them. The guilt of Shayna's secrets and the scars
from her loss causes her to continue pushing him away.

When Greg is offered a job in another state, he looks to Shayna to
give him a reason to stay. Her rejection causes Greg to pack up his
things and move, leaving Shayna even more heartbroken and
confused.

Will Shayna allow herself to love again before it's too late? Find out in book two of the King Sisters series, *Are You That Somebody Greg & Shayna's Love Story.*

ACKNOWLEDGMENTS

Thank you to everyone who supported my first novel! I am over-whelmed with the love and support that I have received since my first release. I am so thankful to have this opportunity to share what I love with the lovers out there! Shout out to my pen sister Asia Moniqué! It was because of you I took a chance on becoming published. Thank you, Basia! Thank you to the entire Major Key Publishing family. You guys are always supportive, and I love being a part of the team!

Mad love to everyone who came out to every book event, who shared a post, or who encouraged me when I wanted to give up. I want to give a personal thank you to my aunt Sheila, who went hard for me on my first book. She was definitely my biggest supporter. I love you!

I promised to name a few this time, so thank you Jasma, Chaka, Kanita, Desiree', Tonya, Reisha, and Tish (JRC4L)! I love my crew! To my day ones, Charline and Marina, thank you!

Thank you to my son, Braylen. You are the reason I shoot for the moon, baby!

Much Love,

G. Fife

PROLOGUE

The loud explosion rang through the air, causing Shayna to cover her ears and snap her eyes tightly shut. The thunderous sound lasted only a second before Shayna opened her eyes, searching her surroundings frantically. It took her a few seconds to figure out what had just happened as her eyes fell on the body that lay motionless on the cold pavement. Blood spewed from the gunshot wound to his back.

Shayna was paralyzed where she stood. Even her voice had disappeared. Her screams were boiling up inside her as she willed him to move. Her fiancé lay at her feet, and Shayna wanted to touch him to see if he was OK, but fear held her captive. His body jerked slightly, showing signs of life still in him. He began to move slowly, leaving a blood trail behind. The door to his home was only a few feet away, and Shayna's mind screamed, *baby, get up!*

Shayna's eyes searched the darkness, trying to locate the shooter to no avail. They were alone. No one was there to help as life seeped from his body.

"Baby, you have to get up!" Shayna heard her voice, but she was sure her lips weren't moving. She was calling out to the man she loved as he continued to struggle.

Her tears were even paralyzed, dangling from her eyes and threatening to escape. With each jerky movement, he moved farther away from her and closer to the door. He placed his hand on the doorknob before glancing back at her. His handsome face was full of pain, yet he managed a partial smile. Blood poured from his mouth as he placed a hand over his heart. Shayna could see the bullet had entered his back and escaped through his chest.

I love you, he mouthed with the last ounce of life he had left in his body.

"No, baby! Don't leave me! I'm sorry!"

CHAPTER 1

*S*hayna awakened from the nightmare in a cold sweat and her tears flowing. She was freezing, yet sweat was pouring from her skin. She was breathing hard and had to catch her breath. It seemed so real. It was like she was reliving the moment all over again. Shayna walked into the bathroom and splashed water on her face before looking into the mirror.

It had been over a year since she'd had that nightmare and five years since that horrific night. Shawn was her college sweetheart and love of her life. He was all things to Shayna—her first love, her first kiss, her first intimate partner, and the first man to ask for her hand in marriage. Shawn and Shayna were the way most people acknowledged them. Never did they use one name without the other. They were inseparable, and Shayna missed him immensely. A love like theirs was hard to come by, and it was unbroken, even in death.

Shayna's phone rang, and she hurried back into her room to answer. She saw her sister Carmen's face on the screen before picking up.

"Rise and shine, sleeping beauty. Mommy is ready for breakfast."

Carmen was her older sister. She was newly pregnant and enjoying every second of it. Being pregnant was something Carmen had longed for. She and her husband, Troy, had found themselves pregnant after three years of trying, countless disappointments, and too much heartbreak.

"I'm up. I'm up," Shayna mumbled.

"Are you OK?"

The closeness she shared with her sisters was unconventional to most, but their tragedy had changed something in them. They'd lost their parents tragically ten years earlier, and that loss had changed their sisterhood. It was no surprise Carmen was able to pick up on her mood, so she didn't bother lying.

"I will be, but the nightmares are back."

Shayna picked up the piece of paper sitting on the nightstand next to her bed. The paper had detective Norman's name and number scribbled on it.

"Give me thirty minutes, and I'll be right there. I'm going to call Molina. I know she would want to be there too."

Molina, the feisty one of the King sisters, was their baby sister. She was very protective of them and their bond. Shayna shook her head as if Carmen could see her.

"No, you don't have to do that. I'll be fine. You two should go out and get breakfast. I'll meet up with you later."

"Baby girl, you don't have to do this by yourself," Carmen insisted.

Shayna threw the paper into the drawer and quickly shut it before responding to Carmen.

"I know, Carmen, but I'd rather be alone. I promise you I'll be OK."

Carmen reluctantly agreed, and they ended the call. Shayna scrolled through her phone until she found *their* song then marched back into the bathroom to draw herself a bubble bath. As she soaked in the steaming hot bath listening to Beyoncé's "1+1", the tears cascaded down her cheeks. The hurt hit her like a ton of bricks knocking the wind out of her. She was overwhelmed with emotions as she sank deeper into the tub with thoughts of Shawn swirling in her mind.

CHAPTER 2

2 *008*

Shawn held her hand while guiding her carefully to an unknown location. Shayna was blindfolded, smiling from ear to ear, and could explode with excitement. Shayna loved surprises, and the anticipation of what was to come had her as giddy as a school girl.

Shayna shivered with excitement. "Where are you taking me?"

"Shayna, be patient. I got you, baby."

They were visiting their alma mater, Howard University. They'd both graduated only a year earlier, receiving their bachelor's degrees —Shawn in engineering and Shayna in business management and marketing. It was homecoming weekend, their favorite time at Howard. The culture was alive with the boot thumping of the step teams, the loud bump of the drum line, the sisterhood of sorors, and the brotherhood of the fraternities! Shayna had pledged Alpha Kappa Alpha, and while reluctant at first, Shawn had pledged Alpha Phi Alpha.

Shayna could hear the hushed whispers of people around them but couldn't make out where she could possibly be. When they reached their destination, Shawn pulled her close to him but didn't remove her blindfold right away. She first heard the melodic humming before hearing the operatic voices begin to sing "When I Fall in Love." Shawn removed her blindfold, and she was standing on the fifty-yard line with her AKA sisters and Shawn's Alpha brothers surrounding her. Their hands were perfectly placed together. Her sisters wore their green and pink with pearls, and the guys sported their all black with metallic gold gloves. The sound of the Alpha's voices matched the harmonic humming of the AKA's to perfection. It was the most beautiful sight Shayna had ever witnessed.

She surveyed the crowd and noticed they were on the field during the big game. She began to cry as Shawn dropped to one knee and held out a ring box to her. Flashes invaded their space, but Shayna's eyes stayed trained on Shawn.

"My beautiful Shayna Shayn, you are the most amazing creature to walk God's earth. We've been together since we were kids and have grown into adulthood together. They told us we would become tired of each other, but I'm still excited every day I get a chance to be with you. There is no Shawn without Shayn, and I would love to spend the rest of my forever with you as my wife. Will you marry me, baby?"

Shayna fell to her knees and into his arms while nodding yes. She could not find her voice through the tears. The crowd roared as the bass of the drum kicked in, and confetti filled the air. She laughed as the energetic, "Skee Wee," filled the air from her sorors. Shayna threw up their signature hand signal, pinky up while her thumb held down her pointer, index, and ring fingers. The cheers grew louder. It was the most amazing feeling Shayna had ever felt. In one moment, Shawn had embodied everything they were as a unit, and she would never be able to replace how he made her feel that day.

~

Present

The smell of spiced Chai tea assaulted Shayna's nose as she stepped out of the bath and dried off. The familiar scent caused her stomach to rumble as she envisioned herself taking a sip with a side of turkey bacon she was sure Carmen brought along with the tea. She

6

hadn't heard them come in, but she was sure her sisters were in the kitchen fixing breakfast like they lived there. Shayna threw on an oversized sweatshirt and leggings and pulled her freshly blown-out hair back into a pony tail. She looked in the mirror, and her eyes were puffy and swollen, but there was very little she could do about it.

"We should really revisit our key exchange system," Shayna said, entering the kitchen. Just as she suspected, Carmen was at the stove frying up turkey bacon, and three cups of Chai tea sat on the breakfast island. Shayna took a seat in front of one of the cups and took a sip, allowing the warm liquid to sooth her.

"I've been saying this for years," Molina added.

"Well, I don't. I like being able to come and go as I please. You two only have one floor separating you, but I live way across town. This makes me feel like I'm still in the sister circle," Carmen whined.

"No one told you to marry the man of your dreams and move out of the condos, Mrs. Black. We had the perfect set-up. We all owned our own space, living in the same building."

"Yes, and that's why Troy wasn't having it. He got enough of y'all all up in our business while we were dating. And that's Mrs. King-Black. I'm hyphenated. Thank you."

Carmen placed a few pieces of bacon on a plate and put them in front of Shayna. She loved the fact that although she knew she looked a mess and they knew about the nightmare she'd had, they weren't focused on it. They were just there. Even though she said she wanted to be alone, they were not going to allow her to feel lonely.

"I say after breakfast we get out of here and go baby shopping."

"I will if you tell us the sex of the baby," Molina replied to Carmen.

"We all know it's a girl," Shayna added. She and Molina had gone back and forth over the gender since learning Carmen was pregnant, so it was no surprise Molina wanted a boy, and Shayna's heart was set on a girl. Troy and Carmen only hoped for a healthy baby, and they'd agreed not to learn the sex before delivery.

"How can I tell you something I myself don't know? We can shop for a gender-neutral baby."

"Yeah, but it won't be as fun, and besides, I think my nephew would love a little barn yard themed nursery," Molina said, placing emphasis on the word "nephew."

"Girls can enjoy farm animals," Carmen chided, and Molina wrinkled her nose.

"Whatever. I have to stop by the studio and drop off a backdrop to Troy, but after that, we're free."

Shayna shifted in her seat, being careful not to let on that the thought of going to the studio and possibly seeing Greg got to her. Greg Navarro was a talented and well sought-after photographer in San Diego where they resided. Troy and Greg were business partners, and together, they were building quite the reputation in the city. Their business was thriving. Navarro and Black Photography was definitely on the rise, and the city and surrounding areas had taken notice. Mr. Navarro had been a distraction to Shayna since she'd met him six months earlier, and it was a distraction she didn't want or need.

CHAPTER 3

*C*armen eased her Escalade into the parking space reserved just for her. She mumbled something inaudible under her breath, and Shayna and Molina snickered, knowing she hated driving the oversized vehicle. Troy had purchased it when they first found out they were having a baby and forced her to drive it so she would be comfortable once the baby arrived. After placing the truck in park and unlocking the doors, the sisters jumped out.

Shayna noticed she and Molina wore matching color schemes as they often did without trying. Molina had on a denim top with white distressed skinny jeans. Her shirt was tied at the waist, showing off her curvaceous frame while her feet were adorned in nude pumps. Shayna had traded in her leggings and oversized sweatshirt for loose fitting denim pants with a white top. As always, she wore understated earrings and flat shoes. She was the tallest of the sisters and hated her height in heels. Carmen's attire was as free and as vintage as she was. She wore a long flowing maxi skirt, simple light green tank, with multi colored beads around her neck and bangle bracelets adorning both wrists. She wore her huge curly afro big, free, and untamed. Carmen was a walking piece of art. She was a show stopper in her own right and carried herself like the art she sculpted. She was definitely a human conversation piece, and strangers were drawn to her authenticity.

Troy stepped out of the studio to meet his wife, kissing her on the forehead. Shayna loved their love. Carmen's relationship with Troy was the most romantic and heartfelt union Shayna ever witnessed. To be around them felt like you were a part of something special.

"Carmen, you should have called me. I would have helped you out of the truck, love."

"I know, and that's why I didn't call. You don't have to do that, mfalme wangu," Carmen said, slipping in some Swahili. She loved calling Troy her king in other languages. Yes, they were too much. Troy hugged Shayna and Molina before they entered the studio. Shayna glanced around the open floor plan and noticed it was empty.

"Looking for someone?" Molina asked, sneaking up behind her and causing Shayna to jump.

"No, I was simply admiring the studio."

"Liar," Molina taunted. "You've been here a million times. What's there to admire?"

Shayna rolled her eyes. Her sisters had been teasing her about Greg for months.

"Listen, I don't see what the problem is. Greg is a very attractive man and a gentleman, I might add."

Shayna was not about to argue the facts Molina just stated. Greg Navarro had given special meaning to the words tall, dark, and handsome. His muscled, lean body was a giveaway to the fact he worked out consistently. Upon meeting him for the first time, Shayna was drawn to his ebony skin, his full and thick lips, and his unusually long eyelashes. He kept his hair cut low and his face free of facial hair just the way she liked it.

"If you think he's all that, why don't you date him?"

"Because, I could never date a man without facial hair. I don't trust them," Molina countered, and Carmen laughed as she approached, catching the end of their conversation.

"You are so right about that, sister," she added, high fiving Molina.

"That is such a superficial thing to say."

"All facts, sister," Carmen continued.

"What does it matter anyway? I'm not interested in Greg," Shayna said adamantly.

"That's unfortunate..."

Everyone's attention swung toward Greg, who had snuck in unnoticed and stood next to Troy, who was trying to hold back a smirk. Greg watched Shayna intently with a twinkle in his eyes.

"I-I didn't mean that. I mean, I..." Shayna stammered, trying to form some sort of explanation.

She was breathless with the awareness of him as Greg stood before them. Shayna took in his large broad hands, following them up his muscular forearms to biceps that bulged against the black t-shirt he wore. The way the material stretched across his broad shoulders led Shayna to his handsome face that showcased his dark skin, defined cheekbones, and fresh shave. He had the kind of face that would stop one in their tracks. His piercing eyes seemed to look through her with each encounter they had. Greg always unnerved her with the way he looked at her. He made her feel like he could see her inner most secrets. That was one thing she never wanted him to know.

"Don't worry about it, Shayn."

Shayna felt a sting when he called her "Shayn," breaking her from her lustful gaze. That was the name Shawn called her. It was a name reserved just for him, and she never let anyone else call her Shayn. Shayna wasn't sure if he'd always called her Shayn or if she was just being overly sensitive due to the nightmares, but it hurt.

"Can you excuse me for a moment?" Shayna asked as she pushed past Molina and Carmen, rushing toward the door.

"Is she OK?" Greg asked with concern etched into his face.

"I'm not sure," Carmen said, following behind her.

"Do you mind if I go?" Greg asked, stopping her in her tracks and waiting patiently for an answer. Carmen and Molina looked at each other and nodded before giving the OK for Greg to go check on their sister.

Greg stepped outside to find Shayna leaning against Carmen's oversized SUV. Her tall but tiny frame looked defeated next to it. Shayna was model thin, modest, and even in her defeated stance, Greg thought she was simply beautiful. She shared the same dark skin as her sisters with big beautiful eyes, and her naturally blown out hair pulled back into a ponytail showed a classic beauty. When they first met, the first thing he noticed about her was that she was so simple, and it wasn't a bad thing in his opinion. Shayna didn't make a big fuss about hair or makeup from what he could tell. Greg was attracted to her layers. He wanted to peel back each one to see what lay beneath the other. He wanted to know what lay on the bottom layer, making Shayna King who she was.

"Did I say something wrong back there?"

Shayna didn't answer right away as she looked up at a billboard with *Good Day San Diego* anchor, Zya Chase, smiling down on them.

"No," Shayna whispered.

Greg followed her gaze to the billboard. "You know Troy took that picture?"

"Trust me. We know. The man couldn't stop talking about it." Shayna paused for a moment. "She's very beautiful."

"She is," he agreed.

Silence fell around them as they both gazed at the billboard, contemplating what to say next.

"You look nice."

Shayna glanced at him for a quick second before returning her eyes to the billboard. Somehow, looking at Zya Chase made her feel bolder, more confident in the moment, and she didn't shrink away from the compliment. She knew, with the lack of sleep from the nightmares and the puffy eyes she'd tried to conceal with a little foundation, he was lying.

"You're a terrible liar."

Greg chuckled. "If only you could see what I see, you wouldn't think so."

Shayna looked at him and didn't look away. He made her forget the scars she held since Shawn's death. Her scars were deep, leaving her with no desire to love again, but the way Greg looked at her with such importance made her forget, even if only for the moment.

"You must think I'm crazy for running out like that."

Greg chuckled. "Not at all. I just hope it wasn't anything I said or did."

"No," she answered, shaking her head. "I just needed some fresh air."

The look on Greg's face let her know he didn't believe her, but he was too kind to call her out on it.

"You know I'm here if you ever need to talk, even if you're not interested," he teased.

Shayna covered her face with her hands. "I'm so sorry about that. I really didn't mean it the way it sounded."

"It's OK. I have plans to change your mind."

Shayna watched as the smile spread across his face, causing her inner thighs to throb instantly. He was giving her that unnerving look again.

"I'll give you a moment to yourself."

Greg reluctantly headed back into the studio to join the others. He glanced over his shoulder to steal one last glance at her before opening the door. Greg knew what he wanted and had no qualms about showing it. Shayna was someone he wanted to explore, and he had plans to make sure she knew it.

"How is she?" Molina asked once he'd rejoined them.

"Maybe you guys could let up a little on the match making. It's obvious she doesn't like it very much," Troy said before Greg could answer.

Carmen and Molina rolled their eyes, ignoring him and focusing their attention on Greg. Before he could respond, Shayna rejoined them.

"The man knows what he speaks of," she teased.

Carmen and Molina wrapped their arms around her while Greg and Troy watched their embrace.

"Alright already!" Shayna exclaimed, pulling away from her sisters.

She turned her attention to Greg. "Thank you again for checking on me. I really appreciate you."

"Anytime."

"Babe, can you grab the backdrop out of the truck so we can get out of here? We have baby shopping to do," Carmen asked.

"Sure. I'll go grab it now," Troy said, walking toward the door.

Carmen grabbed Greg's arm, pulling him away from her sisters. "Can I talk to you for a brief second?" she asked, and Greg politely obliged. Carmen and Greg were quiet until they stepped out of earshot of everyone else.

"Are you about to question me about your sister yet again?"

"No, I'm not trying to be in your business, but I did want to ask for your assistance on something I'm working on for Troy."

"Of course, whatever you need."

"Can you help me with a surprise pregnancy photoshoot for Greg? I want something unique, fresh, and fun. I have some ideas, but I need you to bring them to life. We've waited so long for this pregnancy, and I just want to document the moment as a gift to him."

Greg delighted in the idea of helping Carmen with something so special for his friend and business partner. Carmen and Troy were the closest to perfection he'd ever witnessed in a relationship. He was honored to know them and be included in their profound love for each other. He was honored she'd chosen him to document this next milestone in their lives. Greg hugged Carmen before agreeing aloud.

"I would love to, Carmen. Thank you for choosing me."

"I couldn't think of a better choice if I tried. You are such a good friend and a great guy. If only my sister could see that," Carmen added.

Greg pulled away and smiled down at her while shaking his head. She couldn't resist, even though she'd said it was none of her business only moments earlier.

"Get your hands off my wife," Troy teased as he rejoined them.

Carmen rolled her eyes while Greg playfully held on to her tighter. Shayna and Molina joined in on the playful banter. "Are you two done talking about Shayna?" Molina asked, only half joking.

"I think we're done," Carmen answered, throwing Greg a conspiring glance. Troy grabbed Carmen around the waist and kissed her as he escorted them to the door. Molina grabbed the keys from Carmen.

"Let me show you how it's done, sis."

CHAPTER 4

*S*hayna stacked magazines that had been abandoned on several tables in the café. She loved the fact her customers, like her, still loved printed books, magazines, and newspapers. It was for that reason she opened King Café. She started the business three years earlier after deciding she no longer wanted to be in real estate with her sister but wanted to follow her passion, which was reading and writing.

The thought occurred to her after visiting one of the trendy coffee shops and noticing how many people were plugged into their phones and laptops or tablets. She realized there wasn't any place a person like her, who enjoyed the smell of books and feel of it in their hands, could enjoy just that. She'd thrown the idea around to her sisters who encouraged her to go for it, and she had. King Café housed its own library, offering popular books by renowned authors along with books and poetry by locals. Shayna herself had written and published a few poetry books she kept on display.

The café didn't have Wi-Fi and only had very few places to plug in by design. The floor plan was designed with avid readers in mind. Shayna had chosen to fill the space with comfortable seating, giving one a feel of being at home. The café was extremely quaint and cozy.

She carried an array of specialty coffees, teas, and some of the best sandwiches in the city. They hosted book discussions and open mic nights, but it was the weekly wine tastings that had gained the café a nice following since opening.

"Good afternoon, sister," Molina said as she entered the shop, fully glammed up with hips in full swing.

"Hello, darling," Shayna said, air kissing her.

Molina strolled to the back, turning on the overhead sound system before fixing her favorite smoothie and rejoining Shayna. Jill Scott's voice joined them as she sang "Gettin' in the Way." Her lyrics rested in the air around them.

"It's the middle of the afternoon. This place is never this empty. What's going on?"

"I have a wine tasting tonight, and I'm expecting a full house, so I closed for a couple of hours to prepare."

"That sounds like fun. Maybe I'll swing by."

"Great! Maybe you can help out. Besides, we always have a good time."

Molina looked at her mischievously. "Speaking of a good time, maybe you should invite Greg. The man has made it very clear he's interested. The way he offered to check on you proved chivalry is not dead. You better open your eyes to that man, sister."

"Not this again. When are you and Carmen going to stop trying to play match maker?"

"When the two of you say I do," Molina teased, but Shayna knew she was serious.

"Come and join me."

Shayna grabbed her cup and joined Molina at the table, putting her feet up in a chair.

"How are you feeling? You look a little tired. Are you not getting enough sleep?"

Shayna sighed heavily. "I guess you could say that."

"Is it because of the nightmares?"

Shayna nodded her head and took a sip of her drink. Since the nightmares about Shawn were back, they'd been nightly, and she was too scared to close her eyes most nights. She stayed up reading or watching TV until her eyelids where too heavy to stay open any longer. It never failed. She would be awakened with the sound of a gunshot and the sight of Shawn lying on his doorstep, covered in blood.

"Maybe it's time to contact Dr. Q and see what she has to say about all of this," Molina suggested.

"I thought about it, but I don't really want to rehash those memories right now. It's exhausting, and I don't know if I'm ready for that."

"She is the best therapist in the city, and I'm sure she will know exactly how to handle your anxiety."

"Maybe you're right," Shayna agreed.

Dr. Q was an amazing grief counselor. All of the sisters had been patients of following the death of their parents. They still visited from time to time, but after losing Shawn, Shayna saw her more often. She'd been instrumental in helping her cope with yet another loss, and because of that, they'd created a bond far beyond doctor and patient. They were friends.

"Do you know what brought this on all of a sudden? It's been years since you've had one."

"I'm not sure," Shayna said. She did not want to tell Molina about the call she'd received from the detective.

The tap on the door caused both sisters to pause and look toward the entrance. Molina took notice of the tall buttery skinned man on the other side who was peering in. His tailored white jeans, Rag & Bone T-shirt, and R.M. Williams boots let her know right away he was fashion forward, and Molina was here for it.

"Who is that?" Molina asked as Shayna walked toward the door.

"That is our new musician, Terrance. He's going to be playing live music for the tasting tonight."

Shayna unlocked the door and ushered Terrance in while Molina watched his every move.

"Terrance, I'd like to introduce you to my sister, Molina."

"Nice to meet you," Molina said, extending her hand to Terrance.

"The pleasure is all mine," he responded, taking her hand into his.

Shayna raised her eyebrows at Molina's shameless flirting. "Terrance, you can set up in the same place as before. Let me know if you need anything."

Once Terrance was out of earshot, Molina turned to Shayna. "If you're not going to date, at least take that beautiful man home and play doctor with him. Back in the day, that was your type—pretty boy, fashionable, and a musician!"

Molina was right. She hadn't always been the most conservative sister. She was once considered the most outgoing of the three, and Molina was right. Terrance was everything she used to like before she met Shawn. Shayna laughed so hard she snorted.

"I will do no such thing. I mean, he's alright, Molina, but he's not all of that," she lied.

Molina put the back of her hand to Shayna's forehead. "Alright? The man is gorgeous. At least tell me you see that, right?

"Yes, he's attractive," Shayna confessed.

"You think?"

"Don't be ridiculous, Molina. Of course, I recognize an attractive man when I see him. I'm just not into men." Molina's eyes grew wide. "Or women," Shayna added before Molina could get the wrong idea. "I don't see you going on any dates yourself, little sis."

"Only because I haven't met the right guy."

"And you haven't met the right guy because your standards are ridiculous. No one could possibly meet them."

"I'm sure there's a swagged-out Prince Charming out there somewhere," Molina teased.

"With facial hair?"

"You know this."

"Well, I have to get ready for tonight. I hope to see you later."

"I'll be here if only for the music."

"Get out," Shayna said, pointing toward the door.

"I'm going," Molina countered, grabbing her drink and leaving the café.

CHAPTER 5

Qiana stepped into the café in six-inch stiletto heels and a black pantsuit so fierce she looked completely out of place in the quaint space. Her pearl necklace lay perfectly, and Shayna was not surprised. After all, she was her soror. Qiana stayed dressed to the god's whether she was heading to the grocery store or had an appointment book full of patients. There weren't too many times you would see the full-figured beauty not together from head to toe. That was just who she was. After speaking with Molina, Shayna had reached out to her friend and invited her to the café to talk. She hated the feeling of being in her office and thought having a simple conversation between friends would be more beneficial.

Qiana had been more than willing to meet with her, and Shayna loved her for it. She threw up the AKA hand sign at Shayna as she reached the counter and pulled out a stool, taking a seat. Shayna poured her favorite midday drink, Tokaji Aszu, into a frosted wine glass just like she liked it. Qiana loved the sweet flavor of the white wine. Shayna placed the glass next to her before extending her arms for a hug.

"Thank you for coming on such short notice, Q," Shayna said, using the name all of her friends called her.

"You're welcome, but don't think I don't know you set up these meetings outside of my office so you won't get billed. I will be giving you an invoice at the end of this session. I'm even adding an extra fee because it's outside of my business hours."

Shayna feigned shock. "I would never do that."

Qiana rolled her eyes before taking a sip of her wine. She watched Terrance as he walked into the café and mouthed to Shayna, *who is that?*

"Terrance, can you come over here for a second? I'd like to introduce you to my friend, Dr. Qiana Hunter."

"Hi, Dr. Hunter," Terrance said, reaching out his hand to her.

"Please call me Q," Qiana said, seemingly mesmerized by Terrance just as Molina had been.

"Nice to meet you, Q. I see you're getting a head start on the wine tasting tonight. Will you be joining us?"

"I am definitely considering it."

"Well, I'll be on the lookout for you."

"I'll make sure not to disappoint."

Terrance offered her a sexy smile, and Q returned the favor. "If you ladies will excuse me, I have to go home to get dressed. I look forward to seeing both of you later."

Terrance left the café, and both ladies watched as he sauntered out of the door. Q turned to Shayna with her mouth agape.

"Where have you been hiding him? It's no wonder this place stays full... fine wine and even finer men. Where do I sign up?"

"I know, right?"

Q sat back in her chair and cocked her head to the side while looking at Shayna. "Wait, did you just agree with me?"

"Yes. I think he's attractive."

"Oh, this is going to be good. Come and talk to me," Q said, patting the seat next to her.

Shayna rounded the counter and took a seat on the stool next to Q. "Sorry to disappoint you, but this has nothing to do with Terrance."

"That's OK. Tell me what's going on with you."

"I've started having nightmares about Shawn again. Like before, I don't see him get shot. However, I'm there to witness his last moments, and I have to tell you these nightmares are intense. I'm trying to get to him, but I'm stuck, and I'm forced to watch him die over and over again."

"How long have you been having them?"

"A few weeks now. At first, I thought maybe it was a one-time thing, but now every time I close my eyes, I see him."

"What has changed in your life in the last few weeks?"

"I haven't told my sisters, but I received a call from the detective that was handling Shawn's case. They are reopening the case due to new information they recently received. It just feels like it's happening all over again."

"Did they mention what information they received?"

Shayna shook her head in response. "No, I was lucky to get that information. His family didn't even tell me. The detective remembered me and reached out, knowing the family probably wouldn't."

"Why haven't you told your sisters?"

"Because I don't want them to worry about me."

"That's what family and friends are for, Shayna. Don't shut your sisters out. They love you."

"I love them too, and that's why I don't want them to worry. Carmen is pregnant, and you know the stress she's under just trying to have a healthy pregnancy."

"Understood, but I think you should consider letting them in. You need someone to lean on during this time. You know I'm here as well."

"I know you are. I'm sorry I've been avoiding you."

"It's OK. I know this can't be easy on you."

The sound of the door opening interrupted them before Q could respond. Shayna's mouth formed a smile without her prompting when she noticed it was Greg. He walked toward them as slow and deliberate as the smile that spread across his clean-shaven face. He acknowledged Q with his eyes briefly before giving his full attention to Shayna.

He was dressed in a fitted tank top, running shorts, and sneakers showing off his toned legs, along with another thing Shayna did not want to acknowledge. It was the first time Shayna had seen his bare arms, and she noticed he had a tattoo covering his left shoulder. His style was comfortable, but Shayna had seen the man just as comfortable in an expensive suit.

"What are you doing here?" Shayna asked as Greg stopped in front of them.

Shayna wasn't sure if she should hug him or shake his hand, so she did nothing. His tall presence loomed over them and filled the space around them.

"I just finished jogging and stopped by to grab a smoothie. I didn't realize you were closed."

"Yeah, I have to prep for tonight, but I can go to the back and whip you up one if you'd like. It's the least I can do for your help the other day."

"I would love that."

"No problem. What can I get you?"

"I'll take a berry protein smoothie."

Q cleared her throat, causing both Greg and Shayna to look at her as if they'd both forgotten she was there.

"Oh, I'm sorry. Q, this is—"

"Greg Navarro. I know who he is. I love your work, Mr. Navarro," she said, reaching out her hand to him. Greg grabbed Q's petite hand into his and gave it a light shake.

"Thank you so much. Please call me Greg."

"You two keep each other company, and I'll be right back with your drink."

Shayna disappeared to the back, and Greg took a seat next to Q.

"You look familiar. Have we met?" Greg asked.

"No, I don't think so. I'm sure I would have remembered meeting you. I am Dr. Hunter. I'm a family therapist."

Greg raised an eye at her and wondered if she and Shayna were friends or was their meeting a client and patient one. Shayna returned, handing him his smoothie.

"It's on the house."

Greg raised his cup to her. "Thank you. Maybe I'll stop by later.

Molina insisted I come to one of your wine tasting nights. I hear they're taking over the city."

"You like wine?" Q asked.

"I could get used to it," he answered, looking at Shayna.

Shayna didn't miss the twinkle in his eye as he spoke and looked away. This man was not going to get to her.

"Well, ladies, I'm going to get out of here, but I hope to see you later."

Shayna nodded her head and watched as he left the same way he'd entered, slow and deliberate. She felt Q's eyes burning into her and tried without success to ignore her intense gaze.

"You've had two top of the line fine men enter this café within the last thirty minutes. What kind of wine are you serving, girl?"

Shayna threw back her head, laughing.

Shayna wanted to tell Q that, although two gorgeous men had entered her café, only one of those men made her lose all logic. Only one of those men invaded her thoughts all day while Shawn invaded her nights. It was becoming torturous for her. Q knew all of her secrets, and she was sure she could never understand Shayna's desires for another man. Shayna didn't understand it herself.

"Shayna, I know what you're thinking, and it's OK if you want to move on and start living again. At some point, you're going to have to make the decision to do that. I'm sure that is another reason for your nightmares, so you can gain some sort of closure and start living my friend. That doesn't mean you have to let go and forget about what you had with Shawn."

"I know. You're right, but obviously, it's easier said than done."

"Because you haven't forgiven yourself."

Shayna closed her eyes tightly and rubbed her throbbing temples. She opened them and looked at Q. "I don't know how to do that, Q."

"I know, Shayna. It'll come. I promise."

"Have I thanked you for taking time out of your super busy schedule to come and see me?"

Q smiled at her softly. "Yes, and I understand if you don't want to talk about it anymore."

"It's not like that. It's almost time to open for the night, and I could have you here all night on this subject. Are you staying?"

"You know I am. I am not missing wine and fine night!"

"Wine and fine night?" Shayna repeated, laughing. "Girl, get back here and help me," Shayna said as she walked to the back of the café.

"I am not dressed to be the help, darling."

Shayna threw a dish towel in her direction, and Q caught it.

"Grab an apron, and get to work!"

CHAPTER 6

*T*errance sat at the back of the café, playing a jazzy tune by Daniel Caesar. The café was at full capacity as different brands of cabernet sauvignon, pinot noir, chardonnay, and merlot flowed endlessly. Shayna was glad she'd called for a full staff since the crowd of people did not seem to be dying down.

"Shayna King, you have arrived, girlfriend," Q said as she sipped from the half full wine glass she held in her hand. "I was not wrong when I said wine and fine. The men, food, and wine are all delicious."

"Cheers to that," Molina said, lifting her glass to Q. "I have to admit I was upset when Shayna decided to leave the real estate firm to open this place, but this is obviously what you were supposed to be doing, sis."

"Thank you, and I never knew you were upset. You always seemed so supportive, and you and Carmen convinced me to go for it."

"Yes, I know because that's what I was supposed to do. I support you, but I miss working alongside my sister."

Shayna smiled at Molina and pulled her into an embrace.

"Enough already. I need you to introduce me to one of these handsome men around here," Q said.

"I can tell you have your eye on someone. Who is the lucky man?" Molina asked.

Q scanned the room with her eyes and smiled.

"That one."

Molina and Shayna followed her gaze which had landed on Greg, and Molina looked at Shayna, brows raised.

"Mr. Navarro has got to be one of the finest men I've set my eyes on in a while, and I'm very interested in getting to know every inch of him. I wonder if he's single."

"I'm pretty sure he is."

Shayna wanted to glare at Molina, who was stifling a laugh, but she sipped on her wine instead. She'd felt Greg's gaze on her all evening and had remained busy because of it. She didn't want to focus on the strong desire she had to be near him and used the crowd to stay as far away as possible. He hadn't made it easy as he watched her from across the room. He'd changed into a nice pair of jeans and lazy button down. The man could wear just about anything or nothing at all and still look like a million bucks. Shayna's skin flushed at the thought of his toned bare body. She took another long drink of wine to rid herself of the image.

"Shayna?"

"What? I was thirsty."

"You keep drinking at that rate, and I'll be driving you home tonight."

Shayna felt his presence before she saw him. Somehow, she'd lost him in the crowd, and he'd approached her from behind.

"Greg, good to see you again and so soon," Q sang.

"Same here. I'd like to introduce you all to my good friend, Drake."

The Al B. Sure look alike held out his hand to each woman, shaking it firmly.

"Drake is an attorney at Drake, Johnson, and Coleman. Molina is in real estate. Q is a family therapist, and Shayna owns this fine establishment."

"Well, it looks like I'm in the midst of beautiful successful company. I'm glad Greg got me out tonight. The keyboardist is nice."

Everyone nodded their heads in agreement.

"How often do you host this particular event?"

"Right now, once a month, but the way things are going, I may start hosting one weekly."

"I think that's an excellent idea. You definitely have the following for it."

"It would be a great end of the week mixer event," Q added.

"How long have you practiced family therapy?" Drake asked.

"Six years. I graduated from Spelman and opened my own practice a year later."

"Impressive," Drake said as they began a sidebar conversation to Shayna's relief. While she had no plans to entertain Greg's lingering stares, she was glad Q wouldn't be either. Molina excused herself, leaving Shayna and Greg alone. She was sure her sister had done that intentionally and made a mental note to check her on it later.

"If you would excuse me, I need to go check on things in the back."

"Looks like your staff has things under control. Could you possibly just want to get away from me?"

"And why would I want to do that?"

Greg smiled, and Shayna drank in every inch of him. This man needed to be on the other side of the lens. He was gorgeous and as close to physical perfection as any man had ever been to her.

"I don't know, but I've noticed you've been avoiding me all evening."

Shayna looked away from him but didn't answer the question. She didn't want to admit it but also didn't want to lie.

"Have a drink with me," he said, grabbing two cups from a passing tray.

Shayna followed him to a small corner and took the cup from his hand.

"To a successful night with a beautiful woman."

Greg held up his cup, and Shayna hesitated touching her cup to his.

"Cheers to the successful night."

Greg chuckled, and they both sipped from their cups.

"I haven't been able to keep my eyes off of you all night."

Shayna coughed as the wine got caught in her throat and the comment caught in her head.

"Excuse me?"

"I think you heard me."

He was giving her the look again. Shayna locked eyes with him, trying not to get caught up in his lustful gaze. She thought it was time to let him know she was not interested in a relationship or dating. She placed her empty wine glass on the table.

"Greg, I'm sorry if I've led you on or made you feel like something was happening between us, but I am not interested in dating right now or ever for that matter."

Greg raised an eyebrow at her comment.

"Ever?"

Shayna shook her head.

"What could possibly make a woman lose her desire for love and companionship?"

"It's a choice I made a long time ago."

Shayna was approached by one of her staff before Greg could ask a follow up question.

"Excuse me. I have to go to the back. Thank you for coming out tonight."

"Shayna?"

"Yeah?"

"It's already happening between us."

Shayna watched the smile slowly spread across his face and instantly sucked on her bottom lip as Greg watched in quiet amusement.

CHAPTER 7

*G*reg pulled into his parents' driveway, allowing the car to run for a moment before he cut the ignition. The impressive estate was situated on a cul-de-sac in the prestigious gated community of Salviati Sante Fe Valley. While modest in comparison to the home they'd grown up in, the private resort-caliber grounds with beautiful pool and spa still offered nothing but luxury.

Greg hadn't seen his parents in almost a month, yet he wasn't looking forward to this visit. He felt more obligated to see them than a true desire to be in their presence. His parents weren't the most likable people, and they seemed to only tolerate him, so Greg didn't feel bad about not wanting to be near them. His parents were both surgeons and wanted him to become a surgeon as well, but Greg had chosen a different path, one that clearly disappointed his parents. His older brother, Gavin, on the other hand, was also a surgeon, and he was the golden child and the apple of his mother's eye. He could do no wrong, and she made sure Greg knew it.

"Son, what are you doing still sitting in the car?" his father asked as he approached. He looked like he'd been cleaning the pool, something he did to relax. Somehow, Greg had missed him when he pulled onto the grounds.

"I was finishing up a call," Greg lied, shutting off the ignition and stepping out of the car.

"You shouldn't leave your car running like that, son. It's bad for the environment," Caroline said, also approaching. It was obvious she'd been resting by the pool while his father cleaned it. Greg followed them into the house.

"I'll be sure to remember the next time, Mother," he answered, trying to hold back the sarcasm that came oozing out of his mouth.

"It's been a while, son. How are things going?" his father asked.

"All is well. I spoke to Gavin, and he's packed and ready to move back."

"Isn't it exciting, and he's going to be the lead surgeon at Pines Pediatrics." His mother beamed.

"No one's more excited than I am, Mother," Greg countered. He was thrilled his brother was returning to San Diego, and although his parents favored his brother over him, Gavin never made him feel second best. Gavin was more than his brother. He was his best friend and biggest supporter. When his parents had begged him to practice medicine, it was Gavin who convinced him to follow his heart.

"How are things going with your photography?" his father asked. Greg didn't miss his mother's eye roll but chose not to address it.

"Things are going quite nicely, Dad. Thanks for asking."

"What brings you by?" Caroline asked as she took a seat in the massive sitting area.

"I was stopping by to check on you guys, making sure you were OK."

"That is nice of you. Will you be joining us for dinner? I can have Julie set another place for you."

"No, that won't be necessary. I have work to do."

"Are you sure? It's been weeks since you've stopped by, and you're already in a hurry to leave."

"Sorry, Mother. I've just been busy with work. That's all."

"How are Troy and his wife? What's her name?"

"Her name is Carmen, and they're fine. As a matter of fact, they're expecting their first child."

"Well, isn't that nice? I look forward to the day I have grandchildren. Her parents must be over the moon."

"No, Mother. Her parents are actually no longer living. Why aren't you having this conversation with Gavin? He's the oldest."

"Gavin is much too busy to settle down right now."

"That's right. He has a 'real' job."

"He saves lives for a living, Greg. I'm sorry if you don't understand how important that is. You had the same opportunities as Gavin, and you chose to take pictures for a living."

Greg laughed, even though there was absolutely nothing to laugh about.

"I can't believe we're having this conversation," he said, rubbing his temples.

"When was the last time you talked to Arie? I saw her in *Black Excellence Magazine,* and she looks amazing."

"It's been over a year. I stop by to see her parents from time to time, and they're doing well."

"Well, that's noble of you. Maybe you should give her a call to check on her."

Greg chuckled. There was once a time when Arie was his mother's least favorite person. Suddenly, she wanted him to call and check on her.

"Maybe I'll do that, and I'll be sure to tell her you said hello."

CHAPTER 8

*C*armen was lying in bed with her hand resting on her protruding belly. She trailed the newly formed line that ran from the top of her belly, through her belly button, and stopped right before her pelvic area. Carmen adored that line; it was the sign life was growing inside her, a sign she'd anticipated for way too long. She'd never felt love so strong for someone she didn't know and couldn't wait to meet the person who had stolen her heart.

Their journey to parenthood had been a tough one. They'd shed many tears and shared many sleepless nights and so much heartbreak that it was starting to weigh on them both. To see that little line was a sign of how faithful they'd been throughout their journey, and the little life on the inside was their reward.

"Mind if I join you?" Troy asked, and Carmen gazed up at him. She smiled as he lazily leaned against the door frame, watching her from afar. The sight of him still gave her butterflies. Troy's eyes held an intensity and honesty that made most people uncomfortable, yet they were so gentle when they rested upon her. Troy was a gentleman, a man of great spirit and noble ways. He was an alpha male and so damn comfortable in his own skin. It drove women crazy.

"I would like that very much."

He sauntered toward her and took a seat at the foot of the bed. He placed her feet in his lap and began to gently massage them.

"Umm, now that feels amazing."

Troy chuckled.

"How are you and TJ doing?" he asked, using the name he'd already chosen for a son he decided they were having. Troy was adamant about having a junior if the baby was a boy and had chosen TJ as a nickname. They both just wanted a healthy baby, but Troy felt she was carrying a boy.

Carmen's head rested on the pillow with her eyes closed as Troy deepened the massage on her foot.

"We're both doing fine. Baby has been a little busy today, making it hard for me to relax."

"Well, relax now, and let me take care of you. I know TJ will listen to Daddy." Troy placed his mouth to her belly.

"Listen up, son. Mommy needs to get some rest, so chill out. Alright?" he spoke as if the baby would really listen. Carmen giggled.

"I wish. You know I have that thing today."

"Oh yeah, the one you won't tell me about. I told you to cancel. You've been at the art studio all day, and now you want to run out again?"

"I have to. It's important. I'm really not all that tired. I've been at the studio sculpting, and it relaxes me when baby isn't break dancing in my tummy."

Troy released her foot and slowly crawled to her end of the bed.

"Well, if you're not tired, I definitely have something you can work on." He growled.

"Pregnancy sure does agree with you, Mrs. King-Black." He kissed her lips then placed kisses along her neck, hitting the spot that got her juices flowing. Carmen palmed his head, not wanting him to move as the heat began to rise in her. It didn't take much for him to turn her on. The love she had for this man was so pure that the mere presence of him was all she needed to be ready for him.

Something about being pregnant made Carmen feel sexier. She enjoyed walking around the house naked and watching her body slowly develop as it housed the little life growing on the inside of her. Her breasts were fuller, hips was rounder, and the desire that her husband held in his eyes for her made her want to purr like a kitten.

Carmen slowly straddled him and peered down into hungry eyes that were blazing with lust for her. She removed the kimono she was wearing, the only piece of clothing that was keeping her body hidden. Troy palmed both of her full breasts in his hands. She'd grown a full cup size, and he couldn't get enough of them. The tenderness as his thumb swept her nipple caused Carmen's body to shudder. Troy kissed her belly before bringing one full breast to his mouth, swirling his tongue around her sore nipple gently. The sensation had Carmen melting into him as she felt his erection pressing against her belly.

"I'm ready, baby," she moaned. Troy chuckled.

"Not yet."

He released her breast just long enough to release himself from his pants. Carmen loved the sight of him—full, chocolate, thick, and throbbing. She wrapped her hand around his thickness and began massaging it, inch by growing inch. She wanted to bring him as much pleasure as he was bringing her with his tongue. Carmen needed him to be as ready as she was.

The pressure he started applying to her breast let Carmen know he was close.

She leaned over, pushing him away from her breast and kissed him seductively. She sucked his thick tongue as it swirled around her mouth, causing him to moan a deep throaty moan.

"How about now?" she asked when she noticed he'd grown another inch in her hand.

"Now would be good," he said, swiftly lifting her and sliding her down, uniting the two. They fit together like a hand in a glove.

Carmen watched his face take on a look of pure bliss as she began to grind her full hips, ensuring he felt all of her. She enveloped every inch of him, tightening her muscles. She loved knowing she was the reason for the pleasure he was receiving. Her slow rhythmic winding turned into a bounce as Troy gripped tightly to her hips, guiding her.

G. FIFE

Troy wrapped his arms around her waist as the sound of their love making created its own soundtrack.

"Te amo mi rey," she said.

He leaned back so they were eye to eye, letting her know it was time. It was their thing to reach their peak while looking into each other's eyes. It made them climax harder.

"I love you too," he said as he released inside her. Exhausted, Carmen rested her head against his chest, still straddling him.

"I still have to go," she said lazily as she closed her eyes. They drifted off to sleep.

CHAPTER 9

Greg's studio was filled with the scent of coconut cream and Shea butter as the beautiful brown women stood before him in all shades of melanin beauty. The sisters had skin that glowed and a confidence that screamed at him with every pose.

Carmen had given him some amazing ideas for this shoot, which made his job easy. She'd drawn the African continent on her protruding belly in metallic gold that looked stunning against her dark glittery skin. Greg was amazed at the amount of talent it must have taken to achieve the image to the level of perfection she had.

After capturing photos of Carmen by herself, Molina and Shayna joined her. While Molina's curves jumped out at the camera, it was Shayna who stood out to him. He noticed she rarely smiled when her sisters weren't around, but on that day, her smile was on full display. He doubted she knew just how beautiful she was when she smiled. The yellow tank she wore had to be the most revealing thing he'd ever seen her in. It was still modest, but he could definitely see her feminine frame.

Shayna hadn't been forthcoming in any of Greg's attempts to get close to her, which further intrigued him. Some days, she seemed to be into him, and on others, it was as if they were complete strangers.

This particular day, Greg felt like she was definitely in tune with him as she smiled into the lens. The photoshoot was supposed to be about Carmen and the precious life she held in her womb, but Greg was finding it particularly hard to concentrate on that task. The rarely seen smile Shayna was giving had his testosterone levels up.

"Alright, ladies. I think that's a wrap!" Greg said, flipping through the photos he'd just taken. He had to shake his head as photo after photo of pure perfection stared back at him. He laughed to himself as he overheard them bickering back and forth about the sex of the baby. It was the loud boisterous sound of Shayna's laugh that made him place his eye back to the lens and begin snapping candid shots of her. He couldn't ever recall in the months of knowing her hearing that laugh.

Greg took his camera to his computer and started loading them. Molina joined him, watching as each picture populated onto the screen.

"How did we do?" Molina asked, glancing over his shoulders.

"The King sisters have done it again. You ladies make my job too easy. I mean, look at this shot. This could easily be on the cover of any major magazine." Greg and Molina both studied a solo shot of Carmen. It was one of Greg's favorites of the bunch, aside from the ones he'd snapped of Shayna.

"Greg, I love it!" Carmen exclaimed to Greg's delight. Carmen was a perfectionist and hard to please at times, so the compliment was meaningful.

Shayna joined them, leaning over Greg to get a better view of his screen. Her perfume drifted into his nose, and her small perky breasts rubbed against his back, causing Greg to shift in his seat.

"Wow, Greg. These are absolutely stunning," she all but whispered into his ear.

Shayna was so close he could feel the moisture from her breath on his neck. She was making it extremely difficult to focus as she'd done all day.

"Thank you. I was just telling Molina how you guys make my job easy. The King sisters are beautiful creatures."

Greg didn't miss the blush that washed over Shayna's face at his compliment.

"The man behind the camera is equally amazing," Shayna said to his surprise.

"Thank you," he said, eyeing her suspiciously. It was not like her to be so forward, but Greg definitely enjoyed seeing her this way.

CHAPTER 10

*S*hayna held the phone as it rang for a third time. She anticipated Greg's answer and wasn't disappointed when she heard his soothing voice drift through the receiver. There was something about the tone he used with her that calmed her.

"Hi, Greg. It's Shayna."

"I was expecting your call."

Shayna wondered what he meant but proceeded anyway.

"I'm here with Carmen, and we were wondering if you've spoken to Molina today? She texted last night something about showing Gavin some properties, and we haven't heard from her since."

"Yeah... um... she's still with Gavin. I spoke to him this morning, and she was still there."

Carmen and Shayna exchanged quick glances. Shayna felt her heart drop just a little knowing Gavin and Molina had spent the night together.

Dr. Gavin Navarro was Greg's older brother. He was a pediatric surgeon and had recently moved back to San Diego for business. Greg had introduced the two following their photoshoot the day before so Molina could assist Gavin in purchasing a home. How had that ended with her crazy high standard having sister spending the night with him?

"I was told to tell you guys she's OK and in good hands," Greg said, amused. Shayna didn't see the humor in it.

"Thank you for the update," she said.

"Is everything OK? Greg asked.

"Yeah, it's fine. I just wasn't expecting to hear my sister had a one-night stand with your brother."

"I can agree that it threw me, but they're both adults, so there's really nothing we can say about it. I'm more impressed that they went for it with no reservations."

Shayna held the line in silence for a moment. She knew that last statement was a jab. She wished she could live life unapologetically. She wanted to be more like her sister, but Molina had never loved and lost the way she had. She didn't know what it was like to love someone with your soul and lose them.

"That's not fair, Greg."

Shayna knew he was referring to how she'd given him mixed signals. She didn't know why, but Greg unbalanced her. He made her wish that she could love again. Greg didn't know about Shawn, and she wasn't ready to tell him. She didn't know how to bring the conversation up to him and explain why dating him was not an option. She didn't even know how she and Greg had gotten to the point where they needed to have that conversation. They'd never dated, but as he pointed out, there was always this unspoken thing between them. He would never understand the hold Shawn had on her, and for her to move on was to let go. She was never letting go.

"One day, maybe you'll trust me enough to explain your why," Greg said to her as if sensing the struggle in her head.

"Maybe one day, but not right now." Carmen was staring at her intently, making Shayna even more uncomfortable with the direction the conversation had taken.

"Of course."

Shayna felt the silence on the other end and knew Greg had hung up.

"Everything OK?" Carmen asked her.

"Yeah. Molina is with Gavin; it appears she stayed the night with him."

"I got that much. I'm asking about you and Greg. When are you going to just tell him about Shawn? It will make things much easier between the two of you. Right now, you're making him feel rejected, and a man like that won't take rejection for too much longer before he moves on," Carmen said.

"Moving on would be a good thing. You know I don't want a relationship with anyone. Why can't you all be OK with that?"

Carmen pushed her voluptuous curls out of her face, allowing Shayna to see her fully.

"Because we love you, and loving someone means sometimes you have to be their eyes and ears when they can't see or hear correctly. Sometimes, you have to be their voice when they can't speak and even their head when they can't think straight. Right now, I feel like I should be your head for the moment. You're so overcome by grief and guilt. You're letting the world pass you by, Shayna. Look at you; you're gorgeous, but you won't let anyone see you. It's been five years, sister. You have to start living again. It was not your fault," Carmen whispered the last part, knowing Shayna blamed herself for Shawn's death.

"You don't understand, Carmen."

"You're right. I don't understand that loss, but what I do understand is that Greg cares about you. Without ever dating you, he cares, and he at least needs to know why you can't or won't receive his energy. It's only fair, Shayna. That's all I'm saying."

Shayna nodded, and Carmen wrapped her arms around her. Shayna melted into her bosom, allowing Carmen's love to envelop her.

"Thank you."

"Always and forever, sister. When you get tired, you have me and Molina to be your eyes, your ears, your voice, and your head. The only thing we can't be is your heart. That's all you." Shayna smiled at her.

"Now, let's talk about your hot little sister!" Carmen exclaimed, and Shayna laughed.

"Did she really meet and sleep with Gavin last night?"

"She did," Shayna said, not letting on it bothered her.

"Well, I'm calling her again."

"Don't waste your time. I've called, and it goes straight to voicemail."

Carmen shook her head, and Shayna snickered.

"That's your sister."

GREG PEERED through the lens of his Nikon camera, allowing time for the auto focus to correct and focus on the dilapidated building in front of him. The door was missing, windows broken out, and the bricks deteriorating. It had once been a church, but judging by the look of it, no one would know it. While architectural photography wasn't how he made money, it was his passion. He saw beauty in things that appeared broken. He focused on the colorful stained glass from the window that lay shattered on the ground, gaining him some great shots.

"I will never know what you see in these old buildings."

Greg remained focused on his shot as Gavin joined him. They had planned to meet for lunch and discuss his hook up with Molina. Greg couldn't wait to see how he'd pulled that off. He and Shayna had gone back and forth for several months, and while he felt there was something there, they didn't have a name for it. Gavin had been in town for one night and had already spent the night with her sister. Greg had to wonder what he was doing wrong.

"I pity a man that can't see beauty in something so magnificent," he said, scrolling through the pictures he'd just taken.

"If you say so," Gavin countered as they walked toward the corner diner across the street. They were in what some called the "hood," but Greg and Gavin knew this was the best spot to get some home-style cooking.

They slid into one of the booths and gave the waitress their usual orders before Greg started to give Gavin the third degree.

"She was only supposed to show you a house, man," he said, laughter filling each word. "How, my brother, did you manage to get that woman to spend the night with you?"

Gavin didn't answer as the waitress filled their water glasses and placed silverware on the table. Once she retreated, Gavin began to speak.

"There is just something about that woman," he said as the smile spread from one ear to the other. Greg shook his head.

"You are going to have to explain this. What the hell happened? Is this a one-night stand thing? What's going on?"

Gavin was shaking his head before Greg could complete his sentences.

"I'm too much of a gentleman to tell you the details of what happened, but what I can tell you is last night was most definitely not a one-night stand." Greg chuckled.

"Only my brother can drop a couple of million on a home and start a whole relationship in twenty-four hours."

"I'm beyond blessed, brother."

The waitress returned with their food and placed it in front of them. The two dug in with little conversation as they enjoyed the delicious soul food.

"I need to know more about her. You and Troy have been friends for a while now. What can you tell me?"

"I can't tell you much. I've only been around the family a time or two, but she seems like good people. Any man with eyes can see they are definitely blessed in the gene pool."

Gavin nodded in agreement.

"They seem to have a great relationship as sisters. I know they lost both parents, and I don't think they have any close family that I know of."

"That's unfortunate."

"You know these are the questions you find answers to when you actually date a woman, right?" Greg teased.

"I found out enough. I just thought maybe you had some additional insight on the subject like what type of guys she dates and who she's been seeing recently... those sorts of things?

"I don't know those details about her. I haven't been introduced to anyone, and Shayna has never mentioned a guy."

"How are things going with you and Shayna?"

Greg was unsure how to answer that question. He honestly didn't know what was going on with them. Greg knew Shayna felt something for him as much as he did. Getting her to explore it was proving to be more difficult than he thought.

"At the moment, nothing beyond friendship."

"So, it wouldn't bother you if I plan to date Molina?" Gavin asked as they wrapped up lunch and Gavin paid the ticket.

"Date?"

"Yeah, I plan to date her."

"You don't think you're moving a little fast?"

"Yeah, but like I said, there's something about that woman, man."

The smile on his face let Greg know that with or without his blessing, his brother was going for it with Molina.

"Who am I to judge? You've always stood by my decisions, and I'll stand by yours," he answered honestly.

"I'm glad you're OK with it. I would never want to interfere with what you have going on with Shayna. Even if you can't admit it, I know you like her."

"I appreciate that, but I'm not the one you should be worried about. When our mother finds out you're not marrying medicine, she is going to lose it." Greg shook his head at the mere thought of it.

"Speaking of which, I'm going to need to stay with you for a couple of weeks while they complete the renovations on my house. Mother has been insisting I come and stay with her, but I'd rather sleep in my car before I made that move."

Gavin laughed heartily.

"My door is always open. Molina has keys while she's in and out decorating, so whenever you're ready, just say the word."

"You are a savior, brother."

CHAPTER 11

*G*reg pulled his Range Rover slowly onto the huge cobblestone driveway in front of Gavin's new home. The house was breathtaking. As he stepped out and peered through the massive all-glass house, he could see the view of the Pacific Ocean from where he stood. It was a view unlike anything he'd ever seen. If he hadn't known before, he knew his brother had hit the big leagues. He watched Molina as she directed the movers and shook his head. The thought of her and Gavin still confused him.

"I hear I have a new sister-in-law," he teased as he stepped into the kitchen where Molina stood.

"Very funny, Greg," Molina countered while looking at her phone, obviously preoccupied by something.

"Is everything OK?" he asked.

"Shayna fell and sprained her ankle at the café. She's OK, but the doctor told her she needs to stay off of it for a couple of weeks. You know Shayna is not used to being dependent on anyone, and she's working my last nerve."

Greg was taken aback. For some reason, he felt he should have known about this before now.

"Is there anything I can do?"

Molina shook her head.

"No, she's just being a brat while I'm trying to work. What are you doing here anyway?"

"Oh yeah, I'm going to be staying here for a while until the contractors are finished working on my house."

"Oh really?"

"Yes, if that's OK with the lady of the house," he teased.

"Don't even go there. I'm just working."

"Is that what we're calling it now?"

Molina punched him in the arm.

"Shut up."

"Hey, this is payback for all of the times you've teased me about Shayna."

"Touché. Well, let's take a tour of this amazing home, and I'll show you the second master suite. That will be your living space for the next couple of weeks."

"There should be another word to describe this house because amazing just doesn't seem grand enough. You did a phenomenal job."

"Thank you," Molina said, blushing.

Molina's phone rang just as they stepped outside to the beautiful view of the infinity pool that appeared to be flowing right into the Pacific Ocean.

"Excuse me for a second," Molina said as she placed the phone to her ear and walked a few feet away from him. Greg could tell she was talking to Shayna, and although he didn't want to eavesdrop, he couldn't help it.

"Shayna, sweetheart, I'm going to be there as soon as the movers leave. I promise. I already have everything on your list, and I'll be right over in an hour tops. OK, I love you too, sister," she said before hanging up the phone and rejoining him. Molina rubbed her temples and looked at the time on her phone.

"Why don't you let me take Shayna what she needs? I can sit with her until you get there and make sure she's comfortable."

Molina looked up at him quickly, and Greg didn't miss the mischievous grin that briefly touched her lips.

"You don't mind?" she asked.

"Not at all."

Molina hugged him tightly.

"You are such a life saver, Greg! I have everything she needs; all you have to do is take it to her. I shouldn't be any more than an hour, two tops."

"I got you."

SHAYNA SAT up quickly on the couch, gasping for air. She placed her hand over her chest and felt her heart pounding beneath her hand. The nightmare was just as intense as before, and she had to glance around the room to make sure she was really home. She wanted to cry but held back her tears. She stood to head toward the kitchen and was quickly reminded of her sprained ankle as she winced in pain and fell back to the couch. She allowed her head to fall back but was too afraid to close her eyes, knowing the moment she did, she would see his face.

The tap at the door brought her great relief as she waited for Molina to enter the living room. She knew the moment she saw her sister's face, she would lose it, so she closed her eyes tightly.

"Shayna."

Her eyes flew open at the sound of Greg's voice. He was standing in front of her holding a bag with concern etched all over his handsome face. He sat the bag on the table and took a seat next to her.

"Are you OK?" he asked, and Shayna realized at that moment that she was holding her breath. She nodded her head. Her voice was stuck in her throat. She was confused as to why he was there and embarrassed at the same time. For the second time, he was seeing her breakdown.

"Are you in pain?" he asked, lifting her foot and propping it up on pillows from the couch. Shayna nodded again. It was a half-truth. She was in pain, but it wasn't her foot.

Greg disappeared into the kitchen and returned with a glass of water, handing it to her before opening the pain medicine and placing it in her hand. Shayna took the pills and closed her eyes, not wanting to look at him.

"You don't have to do that with me," he said, and she allowed her eyes to open and look at him.

"What are you doing here? Where is Molina?" she asked once she'd calmed herself down.

"She's still working with the movers. She was concerned about leaving you alone for so long and asked me to come and make sure you were OK."

"Thank you."

"You're welcome." Greg reached out and touched her forehead.

"You're sweating. Can I get you a cold wash cloth or something?" Greg asked her, and Shayna could tell he knew that it was more than her foot bothering her.

"That would be great."

Shayna watched him as he walked around her house like he'd been there before. He looked really comfortable there, so much so that she wanted to ask him. Both her sisters had keys, so it wouldn't be surprising if it wasn't his first time. Greg returned and took a seat on the couch, placing her aching foot in his lap and began wiping her face with the cold wash cloth. His movements were so gentle and soothing. Shayna allowed him to continue down her neck and chest. She closed her eyes and wondered if he could feel the rhythmic beat of her heart beneath her chest. She let out the smallest gasp as his hand grazed the top of her breasts.

"The medicine should kick in soon, and you'll feel much better." Shayna nodded her head, unable to speak with his hand so close to her breasts.

"Can I get you anything else?"

"You've done more than enough." Shayna removed the cloth he was holding, forcing his hand to fall. She couldn't concentrate with him touching her.

"I'm sorry that you seem to catch me every time I'm in the middle of a breakdown."

"I wish you would stop apologizing for it. It's OK. No judgment here."

"Should I ask how you got in, or do I already know the answer?"

Greg laughed.

"I'm sure you know the answer. Molina gave me her key because she didn't want you getting up to answer the door."

"I guess that's fair." Shayna raised an eyebrow at him.

"You've been here before?"

"Once... maybe twice with Troy and Carmen."

"I knew it!"

"We stopped by Molina's place as well, so don't feel too bad."

On cue, Molina entered the living room and eyed them suspiciously.

"You've been to my house without me knowing?" she asked.

"Troy is going to kill me," Greg whispered. Molina hugged Shayna.

"How are you?" she asked, ushering Greg from his seat on the couch and claiming it for herself.

"I'm feeling great." Shayna felt the medicine kicking in, and her eyelids were starting to get heavy. Molina looked at Greg and gave him a smile of gratitude.

"I wasn't expecting you for at least an hour," Greg said.

"I know. Gavin came home early, so I was able to get away a lot sooner than I expected. Thank you. It looks like you had everything under control. You're good at this. You should be her full-time nurse." Molina said the words, and Shayna could see the lightbulb that went off in her head before she started speaking again.

"Wait. You need a place to stay for a couple of weeks, and Shayna needs help around the house for a couple of weeks. Why don't you stay here? You guys could help each other out!"

Shayna's eyes almost bulged out of her head as she eyed Molina.

"Molina!"

"What? I have work to do, and Carmen is pregnant. You know we would make it work if we had to, but if Greg can stay here, that would help everyone. What do you say, Greg?"

"You do not have to agree to this, Greg. Molina is being a bully.

"I don't mind staying. That's if it's OK with you. It's actually closer to the studio, so you would be doing me a favor."

"See, Shayna? You would be doing him a favor."

Shayna ignored her and looked at Greg.

"Are you sure? You really don't have to do this?"

"I'm sure. Like I said, you would be doing me a favor."

"Well, now that we've settled that, let's get you moved in." If looks could kill, Molina would have been a dead woman.

CHAPTER 12

$\mathcal{G}$reg took a seat on the edge of the bed and took a deep breath. He'd just hung his last sports coat in the closet. He'd unpacked all of his personal items in Shayna's spare bedroom and tucked his empty bag in the closet. He was questioning why he'd chosen to stay with her, knowing his lingering feelings would drive him crazy. He'd told himself in doing so he was helping her, but he knew he wanted to spend time with her in hopes she would open up to him, and he could get a chance to know her.

Greg stepped out of the room and headed down the hallway in search of Shayna, but she was missing from the spot he'd left her. He walked toward her room and tapped on the door that was slightly agape. He could see Shayna struggling to get to the bed and pushed open the door, stepping inside and scooping her into his arms, carrying her the rest of the way. He placed her gently on the bed, and she looked up at him with appreciation.

"You didn't have to do that."

"You keep telling me what I don't have to do. It's my decision to make, and besides, it's kind of why I'm here. You're going to have to let me help you."

"That's going to take some getting used to," she confessed.

"Understandable."

Greg looked around her nicely decorated room, eyeing the large queen bed with gray leather tufted headboard, accented with crystal studs. The sheer gray and white panels that hung behind it gave the bed a romantic, alluring feel. Greg wanted to laugh at the number of decorative pillows that sat in perfect rolls, taking up half of the bed.

"I see you like pillows," he teased.

"As a matter of fact, I do. I don't feel so lonely at nights," she said, and he could tell she regretted it almost immediately.

"Have you gotten settled in?" she continued.

"Yeah, and thank you again for allowing me to stay here."

"No problem at all."

"Are these your parents?" he asked, picking up a photo she had next to the bed. He'd learned from Troy about the loss of her parents in an auto accident, but he didn't know much else.

"Yeah, those are my parents, Reverend Joseph and Mrs. Beverly King."

"Tell me you're not a pastor's kid," he said, laughter lacing his voice.

"I am. My dad was a pastor for nearly thirty years."

"I've heard about you PK's!"

"Not all PK's are freaks! That is the most ridiculous stereotype I've ever heard." She laughed. Greg laughed out loud.

"Hey, I didn't say it. I'm just telling you what I heard."

"I'm sure."

"Well, they would be proven wrong when it comes to you." Shayna knew what he said was supposed to be a compliment, but somehow, it didn't sit well with her.

"And how would you know?" she asked, locking him in with her gaze. She watched as he fought with his response. Greg shrugged.

"I guess I don't."

"I won't confirm or deny, but I will admit I certainly gave my parents a run for their money."

"I could not imagine that."

"Because you don't know me."

"I'm trying to."

Greg took a seat at the foot of the bed.

"Tell me more about your parents. What were they like?"

"I had amazing parents. Even with my dad being a pastor, he was the coolest dad on the block. He wasn't strict or uptight; he was a pretty laid-back guy. That man could have been a comedian, but maybe we just thought he was the funniest person alive. He was a big family guy and never failed to show us just how much. He made our childhood seem so magical. He would throw these impromptu parties in the kitchen just for us. We would dance all night. We camped outside in the backyard and took family road trips. I have some awesome childhood memories. My mom was the same, although she was a little more structured than my dad. Someone had to keep us under control."

"You guys were lucky."

"Yeah, we were. Until one day, we weren't."

They sat in silence for a minute with Greg allowing her time to revel in her memories.

"I'm sure it was hard losing them both at once like that. I couldn't even imagine."

"It was devastating. It has taken me a long time to understand how bad things happen to good people like my parents. I mean, they were genuinely good people. My father loved the Lord and served God faithfully, and my mom was right there with him every step of the way. They were devoted to each other and loved their family. I don't think they would have made it one without the other, so maybe that's why they were taken together."

"Do you have any other family?"

"Carmen and Molina are the only family that I have that I know of. Both of my parents were only children, so no cousins, aunts, or uncles. It's just the three of us, but I couldn't ask for a better support system. Growing up so close in age, we fought all the time. Carmen didn't fight as much as Molina and me, but after losing everything and only having each other to count on, something just changed in us. Anything we could think of to argue about just seemed less important, and that's how our bond was created. Carmen stepped into the parenting role and made sure we remained close. Molina showed her strength even when we knew she was hurting. She's the youngest and had less time with them, and she took it really hard. I was the nurturer, and that became my role in our new normal."

"I think it's amazing how close you three are. Thank God for siblings, right?"

"Absolutely." Shayna smiled and lowered her gaze to the duvet. "Enough about me. Tell me about you and your family."

"I guess I should start with my brother, now that he and Molina are dating."

Shayna rolled her eyes, causing Greg to laugh out loud.

"Please, start there. He must be something special to cause my sister to lose her mind."

"I'm a bit biased, but he's a standup guy. I think I mentioned a time or two he's a pediatric surgeon. Hence, the move back to San Diego. He's going to lead the team at Pine's Pediatric, which is pretty dope."

"Yeah, that's pretty impressive, and he's so young."

"And gifted. He definitely took after my parents. Both of my parents practice medicine and are surgeons. My upbringing was the complete opposite of yours. My parents have always been strict, my mom in particular. She likes things a certain way, and she will not compromise on her views. She was not at all pleased with the idea of me being a photographer, causing my brother to become the golden child once that decision was made. She is still not pleased with my career choice. I've never lived by my parent's standards. We had money, but I hated all that came with it, so I created my own lane, and my mother hated that. She can't control me, and that bothers her. I think she tolerates me more than she loves me most days."

Shayna reached out and touched Greg's hand, looking at him with sad eyes.

"I'm sorry that you feel that way. I'm sure she loves you. Maybe she just doesn't know how to show you."

"Maybe," he answered, wanting to evade the pity she held in her eyes. "I guess I can give her that. Gavin and I are extremely close, on the other hand, and I'm glad to have him back."

"Well, Gavin must be more than something special to live up to my sister's outrageous standards."

"I don't think they've known each other long enough to know what those standards are."

"You have a point there."

Shayna yawned, and Greg could tell she was getting sleepy.

"Looks like the medicine is finally catching up to you. Why don't you call it a night, and I'll see you in the morning?"

"I'll be here."

Greg tossed a few of the pillows to the side and pulled back the comforter, allowing Shayna to settle comfortably in the bed before heading to the door.

"Good night, Greg."

Greg looked back at her. Before he could wish her a good night, her eyes were closed.

CHAPTER 13

"*H*ey, look who's up early this morning."

Greg watched in amusement as Shayna stubbornly made her way down the hallway, toward the kitchen. Her hands were stretched from wall to wall, supporting each booted step she took.

"You know I can get whatever you need," Greg teased, knowing she would not accept his help, although it was his main reason for staying with her.

"I just need a glass of water. I'm almost there."

"And how do you suppose you're going to get back to your seat with a glass and only one free hand to hold you up?"

Shayna glared over her shoulder at him and kept pressing forward with every intention to prove him wrong. Greg watched in quiet amusement as she struggled to reach the kitchen. At the rate she was moving, she would need another twenty minutes, but Greg knew if he tried to help, she would bite his head off. The doorbell rang just as she neared the entrance of the kitchen, which was only steps from the door.

"I'll get it!" she yelled. Greg stepped past her to answer it.

"No, I'll get it. You just get your water."

Greg opened the door, smiling at Shayna as she scowled at him.

"Greg, how are you?"

Greg swung his eyes to the entrance of the door at the sound of the familiar voice. It was a voice he hadn't heard in years, but he recognized it immediately. There she stood. She was just as he remembered her; five foot two inches tall in height, petite frame, freckled faced, and red boned. She was absolutely gorgeous. She wore heels that made her appear taller. Her once short cut was now full and flowing past her shoulders, but she hadn't aged a bit.

"Who is it?" Shayna asked, bypassing the kitchen and finally reaching the door. The three stood in awkward silence for a moment before Greg spoke.

"Shayna, this is Arie Daniels. Arie, this is Shayna King."

Arie reached out her slender well-manicured hand to Shayna who accepted it.

"Arie Daniels? That name sounds familiar," Shayna said, repeating it over and over again.

"Arie is the—"

"Publisher of *Black Excellence Magazine*," Shayna blurted out before Greg could finish.

She held tightly to Aries's hand as she beamed at her. "I am such a huge fan of your work. I keep your magazine in my café, and my customers adore you."

"Thank you, Shayna. I absolutely love hearing that readers still enjoy our printed magazines. Everything is digital now, so it's rare to meet someone that actually buys and reads print these days."

"I've built my entire business based on readers like those. If I had two functioning legs, I would show you just how much I love your printed work! The Valentine's Day issue with Barack and Michelle Obama is by far my favorite, of course."

"I think it's everyone's favorite, including mine. It was just as amazing to sit down and talk to them. They absolutely adore each other." Arie beamed as Shayna held on to her every word.

"Why don't we take this conversation to the living room, and you guys can talk all things *Black Excellence*," Greg said as he wrapped his arm around Shayna's waist, helping her back down the hall. Surprisingly, she did not refuse his help as they made their way down the hallway.

Arie entered the condo and shut the door behind her as she trailed behind them to the living area.

"Can I get you ladies anything?" Greg asked as he helped Shayna to the couch.

"I'll take a glass of water," Arie requested.

"I'll have the same," Shayna added before Greg retreated.

"Tell me more about Barack and Michelle. I would love to meet them one day," Shayna continued.

"They are everything they portray themselves to be. Barack is the epitome of cool, calm, and collected. Michelle is classy, beautiful, and so strong, physically and mentally. They are well educated and funny. Overall, just great people," Arie rambled.

Greg returned and handed Shayna a glass of tap water with a slice of lemon just like she liked it. He handed Arie a glass of sparkling water, no lemon, with a straw just like she liked it. He didn't miss the appreciative glance she gave him before he took a seat next to Shayna, holding his glass tightly.

"Arie, what brings you here?" Greg asked.

"I was in town and ran into your mom. I was planning to look you up while I was here, and she told me how I could find you. She said she would let you know I was in town and would be stopping by. I hope it's not a problem."

"No problem at all," Shayna said before Greg could answer.

"Yeah, no problem," Greg agreed. This was just like his mother not to call and give him a heads up she was coming. He was sure she was up to something.

"Are you traveling alone?"

"No. My assistant Krissy is here with me, but she's back at the hotel."

"So, you're here for business, or are you here to see your family?"

"A little bit of both actually. My parents told me to tell you hello, and Nikki sends her love all the way from Chicago."

"Oh wow. I haven't seen Nikki in years. Please, tell your parents I said hello. It's been a few weeks since I last visited."

"They tell me you stop by to check on them often. Thank you."

"Of course."

"How do you two know each other?" Shayna asked. Greg felt Arie looking at him as he sipped on his water, gaining him time before he had to answer.

"Arie is my ex-wife."

Shayna started coughing profusely, and Greg patted her on the back.

"Are you OK?" Arie asked.

"Yes, I'm fine." Shayna took another sip of water from her glass before continuing.

"Ex-wife?"

"Yes," Arie and Greg said in unison.

"How long were you married?"

"We were married right out of college and stayed married for almost two years," Greg answered.

"We both agreed we were too young, and we just weren't ready for that type of commitment. We've tried to remain close, but life, ambitions, and goals got in the way. I still care about him," Arie said, staring at Greg. "Listen, I feel like my stopping by was a complete surprise. I thought your mother let you know I was coming."

"No, she didn't, but it's OK. I'm glad you're in town, and we should definitely get together and catch up."

"I'm free now. If you guys want to go to lunch, it'll be my treat."

"Oh no. I can't intrude. It looks like you guys could use some time alone," Shayna answered.

"Are you sure?" Arie asked, eyeing Shayna.

"Yes, I'm sure. Thanks for the invite, and it was so great to meet you, Arie."

Greg made sure Shayna was comfortable before leaving her alone with the thoughts of him and his ex-wife, Arie Daniels.

CHAPTER 14

Greg and Arie pulled up to Seasuckers in downtown San Diego. Greg was surprised to find she'd taken a limousine to Shayna's house, and Arie had insisted they take it to lunch.

"I love this place," Arie said as Greg took her hand and escorted her from the car. He held the door open as she sashayed through it, and they waited to be seated.

"I forgot about your appetite," Greg teased.

"Aye, this girl has to eat."

The waiter arrived and escorted them to their table. Greg held out the chair for Arie as she took a seat and then claimed the chair across from her. Greg felt Aries's eyes on him as he glanced over the menu.

"What is it?" he asked. Arie laughed and put her menu down.

"I didn't think it would be possible that you would be more hand-some than I remembered. The fresh face... I like it."

"Thank you. I have to say the same for you; you look amazing."

"Thanks."

The waiter returned, and Arie placed her food and drink order, opting for the shrimp and grits, which Greg knew she would. He chose a medium rare steak and baked potato with a side of asparagus.

Greg watched as Arie wrapped her matte red lips around the straw of the island punch the waiter had placed in front of her.

"Oh, how I miss being here. I love New York and the culture, but there's no place like home."

"You should visit more. I'm sure your parents and Nikki would love to see you more often."

"Are they the only ones?" she asked, her eyes daring Greg to answer.

"I could get used to having you back in my life," he answered honestly.

"I didn't mean to pop up on you the way that I did. I hope I didn't cause any problems with you and Shayna."

Greg chuckled and took a sip of his whiskey. He could see right through that line. Arie wanted to know if he and Shayna were dating.

"Although I wish my mother would have let me know you were in town, it's no problem at all."

"Well, we both know Caroline has her own agenda. How long have you and Shayna been living together?"

"We don't live together. I'm having some renovations done on my house, and Shayna needed help while her ankle heals. She was gracious enough to allow me to stay with her so we could help each other out."

"That's generous of her. How long have the two of you been dating?" she asked, her eyes holding his.

"We're not," Greg answered, not offering her any more explanation.

"Oh," Arie countered, cocking her head to the side as if doing so would make his explanation make sense. "I'm sorry. I just got a vibe the two of you were an item."

Greg shook his head while cutting into his steak.

"We get that a lot, but we're just friends."

"But you'd like for it to be more?"

Greg placed his knife and fork down next to his plate and looked across the table at Arie.

"We are just friends."

"I won't apologize for knowing you so well. You want more. Admit it."

"We are just friends," Greg repeated. Arie threw her hands up in defense.

"I'm sorry. I just thought we were playing catch up. I show up in town to find my ex-husband living with a female. I have questions."

"Understandable, but there's no more to the story than what is on the surface. Enough about me. What's been going on in Arie's world other than running one of the most successful magazines in the country?"

"In order to have a successful magazine, you don't have much time for anything else. I eat, sleep, and breathe *Black Excellence*."

"All work and no play, huh?"

"Now look who's being nosey."

"Touché."

"I don't mind you asking me about my personal life since it's pretty much nonexistent. I haven't dated in over a year and haven't been serious about anyone... well... since you."

The last comment made Greg stop chewing and look at her. They hadn't been together in over ten years, so to think she hadn't had a real relationship since him had his mind racing. He too had not been serious about anyone since their divorce.

"I see Gavin is doing well for himself. I just read about his move to Pine Pediatrics. That's impressive."

Greg chuckled.

"Yeah, he's always been the one to seek out what he wanted and go after it. He just purchased a home in La Jolla and is settling in quite nicely."

"I would ask about your mom, but I can see she's still up to her old tricks."

They shared a laugh.

"Yes, she is, but she's always loved you."

"Excuse me! You know that woman did not care for me. She blamed me for your decision to go into photography, and let's not forget the day she found out we eloped. She gave me and my family hell behind that one."

Greg cringed at the memory. His parents had been furious with him for marrying so young and behind their backs. They'd gotten support from Arie's family who'd helped them get started, but his parents had all but turned their backs on them, more specifically his mother. She'd warmed up to Arie after they'd been married for a while, and she couldn't stop raving about her. Greg was sure that was the reason she'd sent her to Shayna's house without warning. His mother had made it very clear she wasn't a fan of Shayna's after only meeting her twice. Once during the grand opening celebration of Navarro and Black Photography, his mother had noticed his interest in Shayna and called her mousy and understated and said she was nothing like Arie. This coming after only a thirty-minute observation of a quiet and reserved Shayna.

"Speaking of parents, one of the reasons I'm in town is because my dad is celebrating his sixtieth birthday this weekend. My mother is throwing a huge bash, and I'm sure they would love for you to come. What do you think?"

"I would love to. Count me in."

"It's a date."

Greg caught Arie's gaze and held it. Having her back in town was going to be a good thing, even if only for a little while.

CHAPTER 15

"What is going on out there!" Shayna yelled from her bedroom as she heard the sound of moving furniture scraping against her hardwood floors.

She'd been stuck in the house for almost a week and was growing delirious from boredom. Shayna and Greg's arrangement really had proven to be a great arrangement. He'd been extremely helpful with her around the house and had even stepped in at the café for a few hours.

Shayna had found herself letting her guard down a lot quicker than she anticipated, but it had returned with the arrival of his ex-wife. She adored Arie, and if she was being honest, she didn't feel she could compete with what she must have been there to offer Greg. Arie was a person who was successful and outgoing, all of the things Shayna felt she was not. She enjoyed running the café, but it didn't bring in the same money she was making when she was in real estate with Molina.

"Nothing!" she heard Greg yell in response to her question.

Shayna tried focusing on the book she was reading by Asia Moniqué, but her curiosity got the better of her. She tossed the book to the side and slowly made her way to the closed door. When she opened it, she was surprised to find a candle lit hallway. She followed the trail of candles that lined the walls to the living room and found Greg sitting on a blanket in the middle of her floor. He stood when he saw her.

"Well, what do you think?"

Fruit, melted chocolate, and strawberry-flavored desserts sat atop a blanket with a bottle of wine chilling next to it. Candles surrounded the room with all of the windows open, allowing them an amazing view of the sunset.

"What have you done? It looks amazing in here." Shayna beamed.

"I know you've been going crazy being stuck in this house all week, so I decided we should have an indoor dessert picnic. We have an array of delicious desserts, chocolate, some wine here, and..." Greg picked up his phone and paused, allowing music to fill the air, "...mood music."

Shayna smiled in appreciation of the effort he'd taken to create such a spectacular ambiance. The candles along with the music and the bright orange light from the fading sun outside her windows were exactly what she needed.

"It's simply amazing."

Greg grabbed her hand, helping her to the floor. He picked up the wine bottle and poured it into a glass.

"Are you still taking your medication?" he asked before releasing the glass to her.

"No, not since the first day." Shayna accepted the glass and picked up a strawberry, placing it between her lips. She felt Greg's eyes following the strawberry as she nervously sucked on it.

"What song are we listening to?" she asked.

"Odunsi the Engine. He's a Nigerian artist, and the song is 'Ocean.'"

"I like this Nigerian R&B. Do you listen to a lot of Nigerian music?"

"Yeah, I like the flavor of it. I like listening to what most people aren't."

"My goodness. You remind me so much of Troy. That man definitely marches to the beat of his own drum."

"So, it's been said. We relate on that level."

Greg felt Shayna's wall lower just a little and appreciated seeing her softness. She looked radiant in the candlelight, and he would forever have the image of her sucking on that damn strawberry in his mind. The atmosphere he'd created was doing exactly what he intended for it to do.

Silence invaded their space as they both tried to figure out what to say or do next. The moment was so romantic, but neither knew how they'd ended up in that space. They felt so much like a couple when the words had never been spoken. They'd never had a first date or a first kiss, so why did they feel like they belonged to each other?

"Tell me about you and Arie?"

Greg lifted an eyebrow at her. He hadn't expected to talk about his ex-wife during such an intimate moment, but if that's what she wanted, he would oblige.

"What do you want to know?"

"How did you meet?"

"We met the summer after high school. She was working at one of those photography studios in the mall. I was trying to find work for the summer and stopped in to apply for a job. Arie was working that day. We started talking, and the rest is history."

"Did you get the job?" she asked.

"I did."

"The job and the girl? That had to be the best summer ever?"

Greg chuckled.

"I definitely felt like the man that summer."

"What made you want to marry so young?"

"We were young and in love, and our parents were against it."

Shayna laughed.

"Two rebels who fell in love, huh?"

"Yes."

"Whose decision was it to divorce?"

"Hers."

Shayna felt her stomach drop just a little at this admission. Maybe Arie was the one that got away, and Greg wanted her back.

"She was the first to say the words, but we knew long before that love just wasn't enough. We both wanted so much, and being married at that age and needing to go in different directions to achieve our dreams was hard. Ending the marriage was just the right thing to do."

"You two seem to still care a lot about one another. Why did it take so long to reconnect?"

"Life, goals, and just stuff."

"Stuff? What kind of stuff?"

"I didn't plan all of this to talk exclusively about me and Arie."

"I know. It just surprised me so much to find out you were married and to Arie Daniels. That just says so much about how much I don't know about you."

"That's just a small part of my life. It isn't the definition of me."

"Do you regret getting married?"

Greg shook his head.

"Not a minute of it. We were good to and for each other at the time. Now, enough about me. Tell me more about you? Any ex-husbands out there I should know about?"

"No, not at all. My dating life has been pretty limited."

Shayna was not ready to share about Shawn, but she'd poked into his life, so it was only fair she shared something.

"Although, I was once engaged."

Greg sat up from his lounging position and looked at her.

"Do tell."

"We met our first year at Howard. We dated throughout college and got engaged a year after we graduated. We actually got engaged at the homecoming game during halftime," Shayna said, smiling.

"I think I read something about that in one of the alumni newspapers! It was the talk of the school for some time. I still can't believe we attended the same college but never met."

"Howard is not a small school."

"Yeah, but I would never forget someone as beautiful as you, Shayna. Not happening."

68

Shayna took another sip of wine as Greg put a fork full of chocolate cake in his mouth.

"So, how does a proposal like that not end in happily ever after?"

"That is a story for another day."

"I don't have to worry about him knocking on the door and wondering why I'm here, do I?"

"You mean like the ex-Mrs. Navarro?"

"Touché."

"No, you don't have to worry about anything like that happening."

"Speaking of Arie, she invited me to her dad's sixtieth birthday party this weekend."

"Are you going?"

"It depends."

"On?"

"If you need me."

The statement was loaded, and Shayna felt uneasy. *If I need him,* she thought.

Her mind shouted at her to say yes she needed him, but instead, she said, "I'll be fine. Go and have a good time."

"Are you sure?" he asked.

The way that he was looking at her made Shayna uneasy. She sensed he was asking if she needed him for more than just a sprained ankle.

"I'm sure," she answered and could see the disappointment that briefly touched his eyes.

"I appreciate you going through so much trouble to get me out of my funk."

"No problem."

The sun had set completely, and the room was covered in darkness. The candlelight dancing around the walls make the room feel warm and cozy. "Naked" by Ella Mai replaced the fading sounds of the last song, and Shayna wondered if he knew that song was one of her favorites. It was the song that exposed all of her fears and desires. They'd fallen into silence, both battling unspoken feelings. Shayna started to feel vulnerable as the song continued to play. He was watching her watch him. They spoke with just their eyes as the connection between them grew stronger.

She finished her glass of wine and stuck out the cup for more, and he refilled it without question. Ella sang, *"No matter how hard I try to run away from love, at the end of the night, I need somebody who loves me naked."* It caused Shayna to close her eyes as Ella betrayed her. She really wanted to love again but knew that you couldn't find love like that twice in a lifetime. She'd already had it once.

"Shayna?"

"Yes," she answered but didn't open her eyes. She was too scared to see if he held pity in his.

She felt his wine flavored lips touch hers and held them there for a moment before she stuck out her tongue to get a better taste. Greg took her tongue into his mouth and sucked on it, tasting her as well. They'd never crossed that line before, and her heart was racing. This was the reason she loved a fresh-faced man. She had complete access to the full lips that he was being very generous with.

Shayna opened her mouth, accepting his thrusting tongue, allowing him to dance around her mouth. They tasted of wine, strawberries, and chocolate. Shayna couldn't get enough as she wrapped her hand around his neck, bringing him even closer. The kiss was hungry, hard, and wet. Shayna was drowning in it, but she wouldn't dare come up for air. He pulled her so close she was almost on his lap as they deepened their kiss and their connection. Greg was hungrily devouring her mouth, and Shayna wanted nothing more than the taste of his wine flavored kisses.

"If I ain't got nothing, I got you," blared through the speaker, causing Shayna to pull away from Greg like someone had poured cold water on her.

"What's wrong?" Greg asked. His breathing was heavy and ragged.

Hearing her and Shawn's song caused Shayna's heart to sink, but she wasn't going to allow Greg to see her breakdown yet again.

"Nothing. I... uh... my ankle is bothering me. It's probably from sitting on this floor," she lied. Greg helped her to her feet.

"I'm sorry. I should have considered that. I noticed you aren't wearing your boot."

"It's not your fault. Tonight was perfect," she said honestly. Although the song had brought her back to reality, she wanted him know how much she enjoyed what he'd done for her.

"Let me at least help you to your room."

"No," she said abruptly, causing Greg to fall short as he approached her. Shayna knew if he escorted her to the bedroom, she wouldn't let him leave.

CHAPTER 16

"**G**reg has an ex-wife!" Carmen yelled into the phone, repeating what Shayna had just told her.

"Yes, and you will never believe who it is?"

"Somebody we know?" Molina interjected.

Shayna was on a three-way call with her sisters. It was the first opportunity she'd had to fill them in on Arie's visit two days ago. It seemed they called only when Greg was around, so she wasn't able to fill them in. After her picnic with Greg, she just wanted to talk it out with her sisters, but first, she had to tell them about Arie.

Greg was out on his morning run, allowing her time to call and get caught up with her sisters. Arie's return was causing Shayna to think twice about Greg. The way that he talked about her and how much she'd done for him had Shayna wondering what this reunion could mean for them. Then they'd shared a kiss that was passionate and long overdue, leaving her even more confused.

"Greg's ex-wife is Arie Daniels."

"*Black Excellence* Arie Daniels?" Molina asked.

"The one and only."

"Well, the man has good taste," Molina added.

"Really, Mo?" Carmen asked.

"I'm just being honest. Arie is a beautiful Black mogul. The man didn't do too bad for himself."

Shayna sighed heavily.

"Exactly! This woman has met the Obamas. She's successful, brilliant, and she used to be married to Greg."

"Sounds like Shayna has a girl crush," Molina teased.

"She's not my girl crush, but I definitely enjoyed meeting her. I was just surprised to find out Greg has an ex-wife, and he used to be married to someone like her."

"Do you think you are the only woman that can see how attractive Greg is, Shayna? Not only is he attractive, but he's also a great guy, extremely talented, and successful. I don't blame Arie for coming back to claim her man," Molina said.

"Do you really think that's why she's back?" Shayna asked.

"I think it's pretty obvious. She's successful and single; he's successful and single. They were once in love enough to marry. Yeah, she wants him back."

Shayna had to wonder if, in fact, Arie wanted Greg back, would he be open to reconnecting with her. She hadn't told her sisters about their kiss, and she wasn't sure she wanted too.

"How do you feel about that being a possibility?" Carmen asked.

Shayna was quiet for a moment. She didn't know how she felt. The kiss they'd shared was next level for them, but she'd also been reminded once again of Shawn.

"I don't know."

"You should probably figure it out before it's too late."

"Yeah, Shayna. From the sound of things, Ms. Arie Daniels wants that old thing back," Molina added.

CHAPTER 17

*T*he scent of Gentleman by Givenchy flowed down the hallway, capturing Shayna's attention. She held the scent in her nostrils before slowly releasing it. She'd become very familiar with the scent of Greg as the days passed. She knew what he liked to wear to the studio, what he wore to hang out with the guys, and what he liked when he wanted to make a statement. On this particular night, he was definitely wanting to make a statement.

Greg was escorting Arie to her father's birthday dinner. He wasn't calling it a date, but from where she sat stuck on the couch, it smelled like a date. Shayna's stomach was in knots as it had been all day thinking about Greg and Arie's non-date. The thought of them out on the town enjoying each other's company made her body ache, but she couldn't say anything. She had, in fact, been the one to insist he go, and she regretted it.

The regret grew to complete panic as she saw the door open to the guest bedroom, and Greg sauntered down the hall with his tailored navy slacks fitting just right. He'd chosen a light blue button down that he wore relaxed and unbuttoned at the top, paired with a burgundy sports jacket. His face, freshly shaven and smooth, was highlighting his defined cheekbones. He was dapper, suave, and smelled delectable. Shayna cleared her throat as he stopped in front of her.

"You look—"

The doorbell rang before Shayna could finish her compliment, and Greg walked to the door. She heard Arie's voice as she let it be known how amazing he looked.

"Shayna, how are you?" Arie asked as she entered the living room. They air kissed, and Shayna took in the overly sexy attire Arie had chosen for the occasion. The asymmetrical semi mini sequin dress fit her like a glove with the deep split showing off her shapely thigh. The deep V barely covered her full breasts, and she wore a pair of six-inch nude Louboutins that elongated her legs. Her skin was glowing beneath the iconic dress that Shayna knew well. The designer, Mr. Giorgio Armani, himself had featured it in the last issue of *Black Excellence*. Shayna had to admit—Arie looked damn good.

"I'm fine. Thank you. You look amazing, Arie."

"Yes, you do," Greg agreed, and Shayna threw a glance at him. He was drinking Arie in from head to toe with appreciation, making Shayna feel self-conscious about her own looks.

"Are you ready to get out of here?" he asked, gently touching her elbow. Arie smiled at him and nodded. She slipped her hand into his as they walk toward the door.

Shayna watched them as they walked out, looking just like Black excellence. She could see why they'd married; they looked damn good together, and she hated it.

"Bye, Shayna," Arie said as she walked out of the door with Greg following close behind her.

"Call me if you need me," he threw over his shoulder before exiting the condo.

ARIE SLID INTO THE LIMOUSINE, and Greg followed behind her. The driver closed the door before returning to the driver's seat and easing from the curb. Greg felt Arie staring at him as he opened a bottle of Ace of Spades Armand de Brignac Champagne that was chilling. He poured her a glass before fixing one for himself and then turned his attention to her.

"What are you smiling at?"

"Us," Arie said, sipping the champagne and rolling it around her tongue.

Greg watched the suggestive movement and shook his head slightly. Arie did look delicious as she crossed her legs, her thigh peeking from the split in her already short dress. Her lips were painted her favorite shade of red. He always thought the freckles on her face made her look younger, but they only added to her alluring features.

"Us?"

"Yes. Look at us, Greg."

Greg looked between the two of them, not sure what she was referring to.

"Could you have ever imagined the two young college kids who ran away to elope would be riding in a limousine, dressed in designer clothes, and sipping expensive champagne? I mean, I know you come from money, but you never lived off of your parents. You worked hard to become successful without their help. Everybody knows me as Arie Daniels, editor of *Black Excellence,* but you know me. You know the young girl who was let go from the college paper because she wasn't good enough. You've seen my tears when I doubted myself and wanted to give up. I've seen your strength when your parents turned their backs on you for fighting for what you believed in. We did this! Nobody else would understand this moment except you. Look at us, Greg," Arie repeated.

Greg thought long about what she was saying. The moment they were sharing was something only the two of them could understand and appreciate. They knew each other's dreams and pushed one another when they wanted to give up. Their marriage hadn't lasted, but they both had fulfilled their dreams, and they looked damn good doing it.

Greg held up his glass to her.

"To us," he said, tapping his glass to hers.

"To us."

CHAPTER 18

Greg walked through the door of Shayna's condo, removing his sports jacket and throwing it over the couch. He walked to the kitchen and pulled out a bottle of whiskey from the space Shayna kept it just for him. He pulled a cup from the cupboard and poured himself a full glass, drinking it quickly before pouring a second. He winced at the burn from the whiskey as it hit his throat. He grabbed his jacket from the couch and headed down the hallway to the guest room. As he reached the door, he heard a faint sound coming from Shayna's bedroom and bypassed his door and stood in front of hers. It sounded like whimpers, and Greg tapped on the door.

"Shayna?"

Greg didn't get a response and tapped a second time. When she didn't answer, he slowly opened the door. He could barely see her in the darkness, but the sight of her almost paralyzed body sent him into action. He dropped the jacket to the floor and placed the glass on the nightstand beside her bed. Greg sat down next to her and placed his hands on her arms, shaking her slightly.

"Wake up, Shayna!"

She was as stiff as a board as he tried to get her to wake up. He pushed her hair away from her face and tapped her face firmly, trying to get her to wake up.

"Shayna!"

Shayna's eyes shot open, startling him, and he quickly released her. She sat up, gasping for air. When she realized it was him, she wrapped her arms around his neck. Greg pulled her onto his lap as she held him tightly. When he felt her starting to calm, Greg pulled her away from him, but she stayed on his lap.

"Are you OK?" he asked, placing his hands on either side of her face. She nodded and moistened her lips with her tongue.

The small gesture made Greg want to kiss her. To his surprise, she kissed him instead. Greg was caught off guard with the way she hungrily devoured his lips. He felt himself losing control, something he didn't like to do, especially in the bedroom. He pushed her away, looking into her eyes.

"Shayna, what are you doing?"

"I need you," she pleaded with him with her eyes, and Greg was conflicted. How was he going to give her what he knew she was asking for without taking advantage of her in the obvious state of fear she was in.

"Don't say that, baby. Once we start, I won't be able to stop," Greg said, peering down into her eyes.

"I don't want you to," Shayna replied. "I need you."

She looked as if she would break if he refused her. He flipped her onto the bed, crushing her body beneath his as she desperately wrapped her long legs around him.

"I need you," she whispered for a third time.

Those were the only words Greg needed to hear before he was ripping every tiny inch of clothing off of her.

She was looking for an escape, and Greg was the only person who could give it to her. The nightmare she'd just had left her feeling terrified and alone. Desperately, she just wanted to feel needed. That was what Greg had always done to her—made her feel wanted and needed. He pulled her from the bed, mindful of her injured ankle.

"Bend over," he demanded.

Shayna did as she was told but looked over her shoulder at him.

"Grab a pillow."

"Why?"

He glared at her. Greg was never aggressive with her; he always handled her gently. The tone he was using with her and the way he was looking at her turned Shayna on. His steely eyes let her know he was in control, and that was what she wanted. Greg was giving her exactly what she needed. She wanted to be desired, to be had, and to release her pain. He hadn't looked at Arie the way that he was looking at her at that moment, and she needed to know he didn't desire her this way. Shayna grabbed a pillow as he instructed, holding it to her chest.

Without warning, Greg firmly and quickly entered her, hitting a spot that had been undiscovered, causing her to instinctively bite down on the pillow. The pain and pleasure charged through her body, making Shayna want to orgasm immediately. She'd never felt anything like it before. It had been too long since the last time she'd given herself to a man. The way Greg steadied her let Shayna know he'd anticipated her reaction. Greg didn't move as Shayna tried to regain her composure.

His lack of movement was driving her body crazy with wanting. She looked back at him with pleading eyes, his steamy gaze devouring her ass.

"More," she panted, needing him. Shayna pushed back into him, forcing him inside her. She watched as his lust filled eyes enjoyed the view. He caught her staring at him and held her gaze.

"Stop," he demanded, throwing Shayna's rhythmic movements off.

They were in a battle for control, and Shayna didn't want to relinquish the hold she had on him. She continued her grind, falling back into sync with her earlier movements. Greg grabbed her waist firmly, pulled out, and plunged into her again, mimicking his earlier movement, hitting that same spot. Shayna did not use the pillow this time. Instead, she yelled out to him, unable to hold off her orgasm. She was sure the neighbors would know about their night of passion the way she screamed his name. She wasn't sure what he'd done to her, but he touched something inside her that threw her body into full orgasm. Shayna released all of the pain from her nightmare onto him.

"I told you to stop," Greg grumbled as Shayna took deep breaths.

"Now, relax," he said, pressing firmly into the middle of her back, forcing her ass to the air. She could tell by his low groan that she was giving him exactly what he wanted. This time, he eased into her slowly and deliberately. The arch she had in her back gave him full access, and every inch of him filled her as he rocked back and forth, taking his time with her. The low rumbles coming from him let Shayna know he was enjoying her as much as she was enjoying him. The slapping of skin against skin caused Shayna to close her eyes and bite down on her lip. She was ready for number two when Greg hadn't had his first. It was obvious he was focused on pleasuring her, and he was doing a damn good job.

Each stroke was deeper and more deliberate than the last. Shayna wanted to say something, anything to hold off her next orgasm, not wanting to give in, but he grabbed her hips tighter and aimed for *that* spot. Her orgasm was so hard, she gripped him with all of her inner muscles, forcing him to release and causing Greg to curse.

"Fuck!"

CHAPTER 19

$\mathcal{T}$he sunlight spilled through the open blinds, causing Shayna to stir in his arms. Greg continued watching her as he had all night. He'd been afraid to fall asleep after witnessing what her nightmare had done to her, wishing that she would let him in. She'd needed him last night, and there was no way he could turn her down, but he never felt more distant from her than he did at that moment.

Shayna hadn't needed him to make love to her like he wanted to. She needed sex, and that was what he'd given her. It was ugly, raw, and driven by need. She'd fallen asleep right after, leaving him alone with his thoughts. He was even more confused than he'd been that first time he'd heard her infectious laugh, and it had caused his heart to take notice.

His date with Arie had been exactly what he needed to get his mind off Shayna and clear his head. Arie was sexy, alluring, and had no problems going after what she wanted. Their date was refreshing and uncomplicated, and Greg loved the familiarity of what Arie brought to him. It was like returning home after being away for a long time. Shayna was complex, closed off, and cold at times. She had a wall so massive he wasn't sure he or anyone else could break it, yet he wanted to try. Maybe he was glutton for punishment, but seeing her in that state only made him want to see what was lost behind her flaws.

Greg slid his arm from beneath her and stepped out of bed. He walked to his bedroom and grabbed his camera before returning to her room. He peered through the lens, capturing her as she slept peacefully, hair tousled, her bare back exposed to him with the duvet only covering her lower body. She was radiant in the sunlight, and Greg wanted to capture her the way that he saw her through his eyes.

After a few snaps, he placed the camera down on the nightstand next to her bed and knelt down next to her. He placed a hand on her neck, running a hand through her tousled hair and kissed her temple.

"Shawn."

The name fell from her mouth as a whisper, but Greg heard it as loud as one would hear a snare drum. He felt like someone just kicked him in the gut as he stood and picked up his camera. It was obvious she was still sleeping, but it didn't hurt any less.

Greg returned to the guest room, placing his camera on the bed. He went to the closet to pull down his empty bag he'd stuffed on the top shelf. As he tugged the handle, the bag fell down along with papers and a few pictures. Greg stacked the papers neatly and placed them back on the shelf. He held the photos in his hand and was surprised to see a carefree Shayna looking back at him. Gone were the modest clothes and half smile.

In the first picture, she wore a tube top and denim shorts that didn't even reach mid-thigh. Her long bare legs taunted him as she crossed them. She had her hair down long, flowing, and wind tossed, but it was her smile that was most intriguing. Shayna never smiled with her eyes, but there, her eyes held a twinkle of delight that caused Greg to smile. Greg wondered what happened to her that would cause such a drastic change.

The second picture gave Greg pause as Shayna, dressed in pink and green with white pearls adorning her neck, held on to a guy who was staring at her while she smiled into the camera. They were obviously a couple and very much in love, and Greg wondered what happened between them.

"Shawn," he said aloud, repeating the name she'd said only moments earlier. He was sure this was the ex-fiancé she'd briefly told him about.

"What are you doing?" Shayna asked as she stepped inside his room. Greg rose quickly and held the pictures out to her.

"I'm sorry. These fell out of the closet while I was trying to get my bag down."

Shayna took the pictures from his hand but didn't bother to look at them. She stood in the doorway with her arms folded tightly. Gone was the warmth she'd recently shown him. The wall had returned.

"We should talk about what happened last night." Her tone held the same coldness her body was showing him.

"OK, I'll go first." Greg wanted to ask all of his questions before she completely shut down on him.

"What had you so scared that you were paralyzed?"

Shayna looked away, and Greg knew she would not be honest.

"I don't remember all of the details."

Greg shook his head, knowing that she was lying. No one dreamed about something that terrifying and didn't remember every detail of it. She was shutting him out again.

"Don't do this, Shayna. Don't shut me out."

"Greg—"

"What happened to you?" Greg asked. "Where is that girl in the picture who was full of life and care free?" he asked, pointing to the pictures she held in her hand.

"She's long gone, Greg, and I don't know how to get her back. It is too complicated for you to understand."

"Dammit, Shayna, try me. Give me a chance to be there for you! Didn't last night mean anything to you?"

"No," Shayna said, looking Greg in the eyes with no emotions at all behind them.

"You're lying. You are just too scared to admit it."

"We had sex, Greg, and yes, it was good, but that's all it was."

Greg snorted and picked up his bag that he'd abandoned on the floor. He placed it on the bed and started throwing his things inside.

"I don't understand why you're upset with me. I never asked you for anything, Greg."

"And yet, I was willing to give you everything, Shayna."

She was visibly upset with herself for allowing Greg to get so close. She didn't want to hurt him, but what she'd allowed to happen last night could never happen between them again. She'd betrayed Shawn by sleeping with Greg. He was the only man she would ever allow near her heart, and Greg was getting too close.

"I'm sorry if I hurt you. I just can't be in a relationship."

"Because of Shawn?"

Shayna shot a glance at him that caused him to stop in his tracks.

"You said his name while you were sleeping. I have to assume he's your ex-fiancé and the reason why you won't let me near you. That's unfortunate for us both, Shayna. You and I could have been something great."

Greg touched her hand, and Shayna wanted to pull away from the electricity that shot up her arm and through her heart. She had never felt anything like that, not even with Shawn. The guilt that immediately followed caused tears to stain her eyes.

"Thanks for allowing me to stay here. I'm going to get my things and go stay with Gavin until my place is ready. I think you're strong enough now."

He didn't know how wrong he was. She didn't think she would ever be strong enough again.

"You don't have to leave."

"I do. I'm done fighting, Shayna. Whatever was or wasn't happening between us... I'm done."

Shayna kept the tears from falling until Greg was long gone. She sat on the side of his bed and gave way to the emotions that she'd been holding on to.

CHAPTER 20

*T*roy pulled his truck into the driveway of their home, which Carmen had affectionately named The Orchid House. The front yard was full of bright pink orchids that she'd planted when they moved in. Every spring, they bloomed bigger and brighter than the year before, making it the talk of the neighborhood. Troy jumped out of the truck and walked around to assist Carmen. She held on to his hand as she stepped out, and they slowly made their way up the walkway and into the house. Carmen took a seat on the couch as Troy propped her feet up. He placed hot water on the stove so that he could prepare a cup of her favorite tea. Carmen was quiet and not at all like her usual self. Troy knew it was because of the doctor's appointment they'd just had. She was worried. Although the doctor had told her things were progressing nicely with the baby, she wanted her to continue taking it easy. Carmen was exactly twenty-seven weeks the last time she was pregnant, and they'd lost their baby girl without warning. At twenty-eight weeks into her current pregnancy, fear was starting to creep in.

Troy placed the steaming cup of tea on the table in front of Carmen and took a seat on the couch next to her.

"Everything is going to be OK. Dr. Dennard said that the baby is fine. The heartbeat sounds good. The baby's size is just where she wants it. It's going to be fine, Carmen."

Troy watched the tear escape from Carmen's eye, and she quickly wiped it away.

"I know. I just can't help but to think about baby Camille. She would have been three this year."

Troy sighed.

"Oh wow, you're right."

"I wonder what she would have looked like and what her personality would have been like," Carmen said.

"I've always imagined her looking a lot like you—head full of curls, beautiful dark skin, and eyes that twinkled."

Carmen smiled through the tears.

"With a personality like yours—confident, a born leader, and a kind and gentle soul."

"She sounds perfect, doesn't she?"

"Yes, she does."

"Let's always remember her just like that. We can tell her brother or sister all about her." Troy placed his hand over Carmen's belly as she smiled at him.

"I know you don't like that the doctor told you to slow down and relax, but you have to do what's best for the baby. That also means keeping your stress levels down. I know that you can be a little obsessed with your sisters, and I hate to say it, but you're going to lay off that as well."

"I don't know how to do that. Molina has this new romance with Gavin, and I'm not sure what's going on with Shayna, but I know there's something up with her. I have to be available to them. They need me."

"We need you too, Carmen. You're going to have to be selfish for just a minute for the sake of the baby. We're so close to the finish line, baby. I'm sure your sisters will understand. In fact, if they knew, they would insist on it."

"I know you're right. I will try to scale back on how much I involve myself with what's happening with them. That does not mean I'm turning my back on my sisters. If they call me, you know I will be there."

"I wouldn't expect anything less."

Carmen placed her feet back on the floor and reached out to Troy for assistance. He helped her to her feet, and she instructed him to remain seated.

"I have something for you."

"What is it?"

"Just wait a second, and I'll show you," she said, disappearing into the guest bedroom.

Carmen came out holding a wrapped gift and handed it to him. Troy took the gift and removed the brown wrapping paper that almost looked like a brown paper bag. He pulled out a portrait of Carmen sitting on her knees, her full breasts covered only by her arm, and her full stomach displayed the continent of Africa in metallic gold. She was looking into the camera with her full lips partially parted and her curls huge and full like a halo over her head. It was a breathtaking sight that held Troy's full attention. He marveled at the way the gold popped against her ebony skin. The photo was edgy, artsy, and sexy. Being a photographer himself, he noticed the angle in which the photo was taken was genius.

"Carmen, this is magnificent."

"Do you really like it?"

"No, I love it. Thank you so much."

"I have more, but that was my favorite. You know that thing I couldn't tell you about?

"Yeah."

"It was a photoshoot with Greg and my sisters."

"I thought I recognized the work," he said, gazing at the portrait. Troy stood up and pulled her into his arms. He held tightly, careful not to disturb the baby in her belly.

"I love you so much, Mrs. Black. You are my everything."

"I love you more, my king."

CHAPTER 21

*I*nstead of going to Gavin's after leaving Shayna's, Greg
decided to go back to his house. The renovations were
mostly done, so it hadn't been too bad trying to relax with all the
noise. They had attended an awards banquet with Gavin the night
before, and Shayna had attended with him after getting the all clear
from her doctor. They still weren't on the best of terms, yet she'd
wanted to keep the commitment she'd made him when they were.

The night had ended horribly with Gavin's ex-fiancé showing up
and dropping a bombshell that he had a three-year-old daughter he'd
never met. To make matters worse, his parents had known about it for
weeks and hadn't told Gavin. It bothered Greg that his parents were
such hypocrites. His dad always preached loyalty to family and the
importance of being a man, yet he hadn't reached out to his son the
moment he found out. Greg expected this from his mother; she only
did things that benefited her, but he was disappointed in his father.

Greg picked up his cell phone and dialed Gavin's number.

"What's up, brother? How are you?"

"I'm still furious. I can't believe Amya would be that vindictive, and
I can't believe our parents can be such cruel people. Most of all, I can't
believe I have a daughter."

"I'm sorry that this happened to you."

"Thanks. I had a chance to meet Chyna today, and she's beautiful."

"Are you sure she's yours?" Greg asked reluctantly. Gavin chuckled.

"That was my first thought, but the eyebrows don't lie."

"Oh no. You cursed her with the brows?"

"Yeah, man. Good thing she's pretty."

"How did Amya explain all of this?"

"She said when she found out she was pregnant, I was insisting that we focus on our careers before we started a family. She was scared to tell me and took off without telling me like I'm that guy."

"Sounds like BS to me."

"Definitely."

"I'm glad that you have Molina to help you through it."

"Yeah, she's been great." Gavin paused before continuing. "Mother seems to think that if I don't give Amya a reason to stay that she'll take Chyna."

Greg sighed heavily.

"Of course, she'd say something like that. She's been wanting you back with Amya since the two of you split up. Amya is a doctor, and mother loves her. She would never like someone like Molina. She's too headstrong."

"You're right about that."

"On another note, guess who I'm heading to lunch with?"

"Who?"

"Arie."

"Your ex-wife?"

"The one and only. She showed up at Shayna's condo of all places, courtesy of our mother. Looks like she's on a roll! Now that I think about it, she was just talking about wanting grandchildren, and Arie and Amya show up. This is no coincidence."

"I think you may be on to something. Dr. Caroline Navarro strikes again." They chuckled, knowing there were no lengths their mother wouldn't go through to get what she wanted.

"How did Shayna take the news of you and Arie?" Gavin asked.

"She's a fan, so things went smoothly at first."

"At first?" Gavin repeated.

"Yeah, I moved back home a few days ago. Things didn't end well between us."

"I'm sorry to hear that, man."

"It is what it is. I can't wait to meet Chyna. She's the silver lining to this whole fiasco."

"I agree, brother. Give Arie my love, will you?"

"Sure thing."

GREG STEPPED into the hotel restaurant and glanced around in search of Arie. Before he could shoot her a text, the hostess greeted him.

"Mr. Navarro?"

"Yes."

"Ms. Daniels is right this way."

Greg trailed behind the petite blonde as she escorted him to Arie's location. Arie stood as he approached, and they embraced. She looked stunning in her all white, Rachel Zoe, wide-legged pantsuit. She had her hair pulled back into a tight bun, giving complete access to her creamy skin and fire engine red lips.

"I'm so excited I've gotten the chance to reconnect with you," Arie said as Greg held the chair out for her before claiming one for himself.

"Yeah, I know what you mean. We're grownups now with careers and commitments."

"All the things we said we wanted with each other. We were young, and we had no business getting married, but I don't regret it."

"Neither do I. We were good for each other at the time, and I've had a great time reconnecting, but I have to be honest, Arie. I'm not sure if I can give you what I think you want from me."

Arie held up her hand, causing Greg's words to trail off.

"Look, Greg, I'm not here to win your affections. I haven't been completely forthcoming with you about why I'm here, but I'm not trying to get you back in my life, not in that way. You know I adore you, but my life is way too hectic to be involved with anyone right now. I wouldn't be good in a relationship."

Greg was taken aback. He was sure Arie was hinting at a reunion between the two of them. He hadn't been out of the game long. He knew when a woman was expressing interest in him.

"I'm sorry. I just thought—"

"I know, and I can explain," Arie said, cutting him off.

"Yes, I've been appearing to show interest in you personally, only because I wanted Shayna to see what she could be missing out on. After seeing you two together for the first time, I could see how much you care about her, and I can also see she cares for you just as much Greg. I sense she has some hesitation, and I thought if she felt like she was in jeopardy of losing you, she would come around sooner rather than later. I'm sorry for leading you on and interfering, but you deserve happiness, and if I could help, I wanted to."

Greg could not believe what Arie was saying. She'd only pretended to be interested in reconnecting with him.

"What about the other night on the way to your dad's party and the 'look at us' speech?"

"I meant every word of my speech. Honestly, Greg, if I wanted to settle down with anyone, you would be at the top of my list. Hell, if I hadn't seen the way you looked at Shayna, you would be the only one on the list. Maybe the time has passed for us, but I want you to find your happiness. You're nothing short of amazing, Mr. Navarro. Shayna needs to recognize your worth."

"You are a sly one, Ms. Daniels," Greg teased.

He was amused, flattered, and relieved at the same time. He loved the fact she cared enough about him to want to ensure his happiness and relieved he wouldn't have to hurt her with rejection. He would forever love Arie. They had a strong rich history, but he knew he was not in a good enough place to give her what she deserved. Even though Shayna was no longer an option, he wasn't ready to let go of the thought of them. Arie covered her face.

"I know, right?"

Greg pulled her hand from her face.

"Thank you."

"You're welcome. You are one of the most loyal, gentle, and loving men I have ever known, Greg, and I love you so very much. Shayna would be a fool not to see that."

"Yeah? Well, she didn't. Our relationship ended before it had the opportunity to start."

"Are you sure?"

Greg nodded.

"Do you want to talk about it?"

"Not really."

"Come on, Greg. I know you, and when you find someone you care about, you take your time to figure it all out. You like making things that appear to be shattered beautiful again, and that's what you want to do with Shayna. I know you're not going to give up on her that easy."

"It's not like I have a choice."

"She'll come around."

"How do you know?"

"Because she'd be crazy not to."

"Not everyone thinks I'm as brilliant as you do, Arie."

"I know I'm being a little biased, but I also know what it's like to be loved by you. I know what I'm talking about. Tell me you and Shayna's story."

Greg sighed heavily, knowing Arie was not going to let him get out of the conversation.

"I don't know where it began. It just happened without warning or explanation. It took me some time to warm up to Shayna and her to warm up to me. We didn't like each other right away." Greg smiled to himself.

"But, when I first heard her laugh, I thought it was the most amazing sound I'd ever heard. Shayna doesn't laugh a lot, so I charged myself with being the one to make her laugh as often as possible just so I could hear that amazing laugh again. It's like chasing a high. Once you've had a taste, you do whatever it takes to have that feeling again and again and again. That's what it's like for me with Shayna. I don't know what has happened to her, but I wish she could see in herself what I see."

Greg paused and noticed Arie's eyes were filling with tears. She was holding his hand so tight he had to move to gain some relief.

"Have I told you how amazing you are?" Arie said before standing and kissing him on the cheek from across the table.

"Only a few times. Now, enough of that," he said, wanting to rid his thoughts of Shayna if only for the moment.

"OK, but I'm not just saying it; I really mean it. You're amazing, and I wish you two the best. I know you would be great together. She's a lucky woman, even if she doesn't know it yet."

Greg appreciated Arie's compliment and gave her a peck on the lips to show it.

"Now, let's get down to business and talk about the reason I'm here," she said, switching gears on their conversation. She pulled her glasses out of the bag she was carrying followed by a folder that she pushed across the table at him. Like that, she'd gone from adoring friend to CEO, causing Greg to smirk.

He sat back in his chair, not sure what to expect, but he was intrigued none the less.

"Finally, we get to the root of all of this."

"I want to hire you to work for *Black Excellence Magazine*. We are looking for a photo editor that will select, edit, position, and publish photos to accompany the text of each publication. We are offering you a full staff of amazing photographers to work with, but you will be the lead. When they asked me who I wanted for the job, I knew hands down I wanted you, and my staff agreed. I tasked myself with flying here to make sure you took the job, so don't let me down."

"Are you serious?" Greg asked, flipping through the portfolio she'd just given him.

"You know how busy I am, yet I'm sitting here. That's how serious I am. I came with an offer that guarantees you a salary I'm sure will not be matched by any other company. We will pay all of your relocation expenses. You can open a second studio in New York and allow

Troy to run the San Diego office. I know how much you like architecture photography, so I've even negotiated a spot for that in our magazine. It's all there in black and white. All you have to do is agree and sign. If you read carefully, I think you'll see I covered just about everything," she said confidently.

Greg continued skimming through the impressive offer she'd just laid out for him. Arie had covered all she'd said and more.

"Wow. Yeah, you've most certainly covered everything. I don't know what to say. You are full of surprises today."

He was flattered and couldn't help but notice how great the timing was. This was just what he needed to get away from Shayna King.

"You can say anything as long as it ends with yes."

Arie had just offered him an opportunity of a lifetime, and he knew he would be a fool not to take it, but there were so many factors that came with an offer like this.

"I am absolutely flattered, Arie. You've made me an offer that is more than fair. I have to talk to Troy to get his input about a second location. He's my business partner, and I wouldn't feel right if I made this decision without him."

"That's fair. I'm in town until you make your decision. Whenever you're ready, let me know."

Greg nodded at her.

"I have a conference call in a few minutes, but as always, it was a pleasure seeing you again," Arie said, standing. Greg followed suit, and they embraced.

"Greg, you can have the woman and the job," she whispered in his ear. Greg shook his head.

"Thank you again for everything, Arie. I'm so proud of you, woman."

"The best way to thank me is to take the job offer."

CHAPTER 22

*S*hayna stepped into her condo after putting in time at the café. Although the schedule was full and she didn't necessarily have to be there, she welcomed the distraction. She kicked her shoes off at the door and tilted her head when she heard laughter coming from the living room. She knew it was Molina before she saw her and rolled her eyes. She loved her sisters, but the pop ups were getting out of control.

"Hey, doll," Molina said as Shayna strolled into the living room.

She was positioned on the couch with her feet tucked beneath her, eating popcorn and talking on the phone.

"What are you doing here?"

"Since when did I need a reason to visit my sister?"

"You don't. I was just asking."

Molina turned her phone around so Shayna could see Carmen on FaceTime. Shayna sat on the couch next to Molina and grabbed the phone from her hand.

"Hey, Carmen. How are you feeling? You look great. You're literally glowing."

"Thank you. I'm hanging in there. The doctor just wants me to continue taking it easy, and you know Troy is making sure I follow the doctor's orders."

"Good for him!" Molina yelled.

"Enough about me. Shayna, I really wanted to be there for this conversation, and you know I would be if I could."

Shayna stared at Molina.

"What conversation?"

"We know about Shawn's case being reopened."

Shayna closed her eyes and allowed her head to fall back on the couch.

"Why didn't you tell us, Shayna?" Carmen asked.

"Because I didn't want you guys to worry. Carmen, you especially should not be stressing and worrying about me."

"We're going to always worry about you, Shayna, just like you will always worry about us."

"I know, but I genuinely don't want you to. Molina, you have your own thing going on with Gavin, and Carmen, with your pregnancy. I've been dealing with this for years."

"Unfortunately, you don't get to decide for us, sis. No matter what I'm going through, I will always make sure to be there for you," Molina said.

"Same here. Now, tell us what's going on."

Shayna sighed heavily. "I got a call from Detective Norman, who was working on Shawn's case when it first happened. He told me the case was being reopened due to new evidence they felt could help solve it."

"Did they say what the evidence is?" Molina asked.

"Not at first, but I just found out the person who did it has come forward. He's already locked up, and he admitted to doing it."

"Why?" Molina and Carmen asked at the same time.

"It was just totally random. Shawn was at the wrong place at the wrong time, and the guy tried to rob him."

"That's so awful."

"Yeah, I just always thought there would be more to the story than just timing. I guess it doesn't really matter. At the end of the day, an innocent man lost his life."

"Now we know what brought your nightmares back."

Shayna nodded.

"I'm sorry, sister," Molina said.

"And I'm sorry about you and Gavin."

"Thank you. I'm sure I'll get through it.

"Shayna, I have something I think I should tell you."

Shayna looked down at the screen so she could see Carmen. "Spit it out."

"Greg is moving to New York. He accepted a job with *Black Excellence.*"

"Wait. What? What about his studio and his partnership with Greg?"

"Arie offered to open up a second location in Manhattan, and both Greg and Troy thought it would be a good business move."

Shayna gave the phone back to Molina and stood up.

"How could he not tell me this? When is he leaving?"

"In a few days."

Shayna stopped pacing and looked at Molina. "Maybe it's for the best."

"You don't mean that, Shayna."

"Yes, I do," she said. "Can you excuse me for a minute?" she asked, as she headed down the hallway to her room.

"Do you think she'll be OK?" Molina asked.

"I hope so."

CHAPTER 23

Greg taped the last box and labeled it before placing it in an empty corner. He pulled out a water bottle and took a long drink before placing it on the floor beside him. He'd been working all morning putting the finishing touches on his packing and was finally done. The movers would be coming in a few days, and he was due to be moved into his new home in New York in less than a week.

After speaking with Troy and his parents, they convinced him the move would be a perfect fit for him, and he really couldn't deny Arie had left nothing to chance with all she was offering him. He'd accepted her offer only after a twenty-four hour wait, and she'd been ecstatic. They'd signed the contract, and she'd flown back to New York the same day.

Greg hadn't spoken to Shayna since leaving her home almost two weeks ago. He thought about calling to tell her about his move but thought better of it. He was sure Carmen would tell her, and he knew she would be hurt she hadn't heard it from him, and in a way, he wanted her to hurt for him.

"So, you're really doing it, brother?" Gavin asked as he entered the empty house.

"It's just like you to show up after the work is done."

"You know these hands are how I make a living. I can't use them on packing and lifting."

"But you can use them to lay brothers out?"

"If I have to."

"Where are the rest of the lazy bums you call friends."

On cue, Drake and Ryan walked in with beer in tow. Ryan was also a friend of theirs from college and was the comedian of the bunch.

"Who the hell are you calling bum, runaway bride?" he joked, causing Gavin and Drake to laugh hysterically. "We all know the only reason you're leaving is to get away from that woman. You're moving all the way to New York to do it. You must have it bad."

"I'm moving because I have another job."

"Oh, that's right. The job with your ex-wife. Take a beer. You're going to need it," Ryan said, handing Greg a beer he'd just opened.

"Arie is good peoples, man."

"But she's still an ex-wife."

Drake and Gavin nodded in agreement.

"Gavin, you should not be agreeing. You just left that fine ass woman to go back to an ex yourself. Something is wrong with both of y'all."

Drake laughed louder, causing all three men to look at him.

"What? It was funny."

"I might have to give you a run for your money on Shayna. She's just my type—beautiful, smart, a little conservative, just like I like my women."

Greg glared at him but didn't respond.

"Sorry, brother, but you would need to grow a few more inches to get on that ride," Gavin said in his brother's defense.

Ryan was a short Lorenz Tate look-a-like, down to the height and build, and they stayed joking on him about it.

"Check you out, trying to throw hot ones. That was a little funny, but stick to saving lives, and leave the jokes to me, doc."

Greg set the can of beer down without drinking it.

"Are you really just going to leave without talking to her first?" Gavin asked.

"Even if I talk to her, it wouldn't change anything. The job has been accepted and contract has been signed. I'm moving to New York, brother."

"I can't believe it, but I'm proud of you."

"I wish I could be here longer to get to know my niece, man."

"I know. We'll be sure to FaceTime you often so she knows who you are."

The light taps at the door caused the men to stare at it. Gavin, standing the closest, walked toward the closed door and opened it. He said something to the person on the other side before moving out of the way and letting in Shayna. Greg was surprised to see her, and his heart did a little something at the sight of her.

"Hey, guys."

"Hey, Shayna," they all said in unison.

Greg noticed Ryan staring at her and grabbed her arm, ushering her to his now empty bedroom. He pushed a large box at her so she could sit, and she did.

"You're really leaving?"

"Yeah. She made me an offer I couldn't refuse. Besides, there was nothing here preventing me from going." He held her eyes for a moment, and she did the same.

"Congratulations."

"Thank you."

"I know we didn't end things on a good note, but I thought you would tell me if you were planning to leave. Why did I have to hear it from Carmen?"

"We never had anything to end, Shayna. I didn't know if my move would even matter to you."

"Of course, it matters. You should tell me something as big as this. Something as big as I may never see you again."

Her words caused a longing he hadn't felt before. Never had he thought he wouldn't see her again.

"It wasn't all bad between us. We are friends, right?"

"Yeah, we are friends. I just wanted so much more from you, Shayna. I was willing to fight for you, but I can't fight a ghost."

Shayna's gaze shot up at him. *Had he found out about Shawn*, she wondered.

"It's impossible to fight something that you have no idea you're fighting," he continued.

"I know, but I told you I wasn't easy, Greg. I come with a lot of baggage, more than I expect any man to deal with."

Greg nodded his head.

"So, what brings you here?"

"I honestly came to see if it was real." Shayna looked around the room before looking back at him.

"I see that it is."

"Yes, it's very real."

Shayna looked at him with a mischievous grin. "Let me take you out before you leave?"

Greg's eyebrows raised.

"You want to take me out?"

"Yeah, it's the least I can do for all you've done for me."

Greg knelt down beside her.

"I will agree only if I pay, and you promise to let down your guard for the night. Let me meet Shayna King."

"I think I can do that."

"Well, we have a date."

CHAPTER 24

Shayna twirled around so her sisters could capture every angle of the outfit she'd chosen for her date with Greg. She'd promised him she would let her guard down, and she was going to hold true to her promise down to the outfit she planned to wear and the shoes on her feet.

"Shayna, sister, I love you, but that is not it. You told the man you were going to show him Shayna King, and that outfit says Grandma King."

Carmen giggled at Molina's comment. She lay stretched out on the bed while Molina sat Indian style on the floor. They were three outfits in, and Molina had shaded every last one of them.

"It's not that bad, is it?"

"I have to agree with her, sis. You really should try to be just a little sexier."

"A little sexier? Throw the whole outfit away, sis. I've been through your closet many times, and I know for a fact you don't have anything in there for this occasion." Molina stood and ran to the living room, returning with a bag.

"That is why I purchased you something myself. You can thank me later."

Shayna pulled the gold spaghetti strapped minidress from the bag and held it to her body. The flimsy material left very little to the imagination, and Shayna was sure it was by design.

"Ooh la la, Shayna, I think that is a winner. You will definitely hold Greg's attention all night in that dress."

"There's not much to it."

"That is the point. Now, go change so we can see how it fits."

Shayna stepped into the room after changing into the dress Molina had purchased. Her makeup was done, and she'd let her usually tamed curls flow freely. She felt amazing when she looked at herself in the mirror. It had been a really long time since she'd allowed herself to be free. From the clothes she wore, the people she allowed in her life, every aspect of her life had been restricted, but for the night, she wanted to feel like her old self with no guilt.

The smiles on Molina and Carmen's face spoke volumes as she twirled around in front of them.

"Damn, Shayna. I forgot you had those legs, girl."

"Yeah, Shayna. You look hot right now, sister."

"You really think so?"

"Oh yeah," Molina said.

~

GREG RODE the elevator to Shayna's floor and strolled down the hallway until he reached her door. He stood on the outside and took a deep breath, wondering if going on this date was even worth it with his upcoming move. He tapped on the door and waited for her to open it. The door opened, and Molina and a very pregnant Carmen stood on the other side smiling at him. He hugged each one, giving them a kiss on the cheek.

"Shayna is going to be out in a second. What do you two have planned for the night?"

"I'm not sure. She wanted to plan this out, so I'm just following her lead."

Greg reached out his hand to Molina and she took his in hers.

"I'm sorry to hear about your breakup with Gavin."

"Me too."

"I know he really loves you, he's just doing what he thinks is best for Chyna. Gavin is the type of guy that always puts others before himself."

"I know he is and that's why it hurts so much."

Shayna appeared from the hallway, and Greg's breath caught in his throat at the sight of her. His hand gently touched his chest when she smiled, causing him to return the favor. She looked absolutely stunning in a metallic gold spaghetti strapped minidress that showed off legs that went on for days. The deep V showed off smooth dark skin that glistened and begged to be kissed. He'd never seen her hair so untamed and full of curls. She looked like a melanin goddess.

"You look stunning." The words left his mouth with no help from him.

"Thank you. You look very handsome yourself."

"Thank you. I brought a gift for you," he said, handing her the tiny bag he held in his hand.

Shayna took the bag and pulled out a tiny box and opened it. A pair of pearl earrings surrounded by diamonds sparkled at her, and Shayna fingered them, admiring the details.

"They are beautiful," she said as Molina and Carmen surrounded her.

"You should wear these tonight," Molina said. Carmen pulled one from the box as Molina took the other and placed them in Shayna's ears.

"Perfect," Greg said, admiring her. "Shall we get out of here?"

"Yes."

Greg led her out the door and to the car. He noticed with heels on she was almost as tall as he was as he ushered her into the car.

"So, where are we going, Ms. King?"

"I remembered you asking me to dance at the wine tasting, and I wasn't so nice to you."

"I remember it well."

"So, tonight, we're going salsa dancing."

Greg chuckled. "I don't know anything about salsa dancing, sweetheart."

"I will teach you."

"You salsa dance?

"Yes. You said you wanted to meet Shayna King, and salsa is one of the things I love to do."

"I'm enjoying this night already."

CHAPTER 25

*S*hayna gave Greg directions to Tango Del Rey, a salsa club in downtown San Diego. The club was hosting salsa night with two levels of dance floors and a DJ on both floors. Shayna hadn't been salsa dancing in too long, and she was bubbling with excitement as Greg led her into the cathedral style dance hall. The music from the live band greeted them as they walked in the door to discover a full house. Shayna, unable to contain herself, pulled Greg to the dance floor.

"We're just jumping right in, huh?" he shouted over the music.

"Yes! Don't you just love the music!"

Greg watched as a glowing Shayna moved around him. Her hips moved seductively from side to side as she stepped forward then back in tune with the music. She tossed her curls from side to side as her hands glided over her body. Greg's eyes were glued to her. He could not believe this was the same Shayna he'd known for all this time. She was vibrant and sexy, and the glow from her smile was making him rethink his decision to move. He could visualize himself waking up to this woman every day.

Shayna placed her hands on each side of his hips, showing him with her body how to move. Greg fell in sync with her as she took his hand in hers, and he wrapped one arm around her waist. Their temperature raised a few notches as they danced, bodies pressed closely together.

"What do you think?" she asked, speaking closely to his ear.

"I'm just wondering who you are and where have you been all my life?"

Shayna threw back her head, laughing. It was the same laugh she had the day of the photoshoot, and it gave him the same exact feeling. Greg nestled his face into her neck, unable to resist. Shayna squealed with laughter as he spun her around, no longer following the dance moves she'd just taught him. They danced a slow dance, no longer focusing on anyone or anything around them. Shayna pressed her lips to his, and they parted like she was the key to unlock them. They held so much unleashed passion that it all came spilling out onto the dance floor as Greg's hands roamed her body covered only in the flimsy material of the dress. Shayna wrapped her hands around his neck, eagerly kissing his lips, neck, and any other place she could touch his skin.

"We've got to stop, baby," Greg whispered. "We're giving people a free show."

Shayna looked around at the eyes that were watching them. Most people held smiles, and Shayna buried her head into his chest. Greg grabbed her hand and led her to the bar as the crowd applauded them. Shayna covered her face as they stood at the bar. Greg was full out laughing.

"Are they still looking?"

"No, now they're all trying to mimic our moves."

Shayna looked out toward the dance floor, and sure enough, it looked like a scene from *Dirty Dancing*. Shayna laughed.

"What have we done?"

"It looks like we got people in the mood to make babies tonight."

They enjoyed dinner at the restaurant inside the club before hitting the dance floor, dancing through multiple songs back to back. When they left, Shayna directed him to their next location, King Café. Greg glanced at her curiously.

"You're working during our date?"

"No, this is part of our date."

"What are you up to, Shayna King?"

"You're going to have to follow me inside to see."

They stepped into the full café, and Shayna held his hand, pulling him through the crowd. All of the seats were occupied, so Shayna led him to the back, and they stood, watching a master poet recite a poem.

"You brought me to open mic night?"

"Yes. Another thing that I love is poetry. I even have a few published books."

"Another thing I didn't know about you."

Shayna smiled and turned her attention back to the poet. Greg watched her as she delighted in every word. He was enjoying her too much and started to wonder if this date was such a good idea. If the thought of leaving her caused an ache before, he was surely going to be in pain without her now.

When the poet finished, Shayna began to snap along with the other poet lovers. She looked at Greg, encouraging him to do the same, and he obliged. The host returned to the stage and grabbed the mic from the stand.

"Alright, we have a special treat for you all. Our very own Ms. Shayna King is joining us on the mic tonight. Let's show her some love, y'all!"

Greg watched as she made her way to the stage. She stood up front, looking confident, sexy, and totally in her element. He folded his arms in anticipation of what was to come.

"Good evening, everyone. I am honored to have all of you here tonight. Unfortunately, I picked the night we have a full house to make my comeback."

The crowd laughed and cheered, encouraging her to proceed.

"I brought a special guest with me tonight. I'm sure some of you know him. He's a very talented photographer here in San Diego. Can you guys make Mr. Navarro feel welcomed?"

Greg chuckled as the crowd snapped and cheered.

Shayna started reciting a poem about love, loss, and second chances. The way she spoke with so much passion held Greg's full attention. He got the feeling that her loss was greater than he even knew, and he ached for her. When she was done, the crowd roared, and Greg found himself clapping loudly instead of finger snapping. He was thoroughly impressed by her talent.

Shayna was still full of energy when they stepped off the elevator on her floor. She removed her heels before making her way down the hallway.

"Men have it way too easy."

"I have to agree," he countered.

To her surprise, Greg lifted her into his arms. Shayna wrapped her hands around her neck as he carried her to the door.

"I don't think I told you how much I really enjoyed you this evening."

"Only a few dozen times, but I'm not complaining. Come in and have a night cap with me."

Greg placed her back on her feet as she unlocked the door, following her inside. He took a seat on the couch, and she handed him a glass of whiskey. She took a seat on the couch, tucking her bare legs beneath her.

"Tonight was fun. I haven't done anything like this in ages."

"Why is that?"

"My life is so much different now. I forgot how to live like this."

"That's such a shame. You look so good doing it."

"Thank you."

"You should definitely smile more."

"Honestly, I try. I can't get people to understand that I really try. When you suffer as much loss as I have, it's really difficult to find yourself again, let alone your smile. I haven't been able to." She gave him some of the truth. It was just enough to keep him from asking too many questions.

"Like I said before, I can only imagine what it's like to lose both parents. I don't have a close relationship with mine, and even I would be devastated."

"Yeah, it's a lot to take on. I think you fight for the rest of your life to get back to who you were before the loss when honestly you never get back. A piece of you will forever be missing."

"I'm sorry that happened to you."

"Me too."

"Your poem was intense. I felt like there was more to your loss than you've let on."

"There is so much more to all of this, Greg. I'm just glad I got the opportunity to share just a little bit of me with you today."

"So am I. It's getting late. I should probably get going. I really enjoyed meeting Shayna King."

Shayna watched as he stood, preparing to leave. She wanted more time with him. She was enjoying being herself with him.

"You're leaving?"

"Yeah, I have an early day tomorrow."

"Stay."

Shayna stood in front of him, waiting with baited breath for him to respond. She needed him to stay with her.

"I can't."

"Why not?"

"I want to do things to you that you're not ready for, Shayna."

"I'm ready," she whispered.

The way she said those words and the dip in her voice made Greg want to give in to her pleading eyes, but he knew like before, once they got started, he wouldn't be able to stop. Shayna had already shown him she was not ready for what he had in store for her.

"I don't want you for just a night. Every part of me wants to be deep inside you. My mind, my body, and my heart... all of it, Shayna. That's what I want from you. Are you ready for that?"

She held his stern gaze, and for a moment, Greg thought she was going to say yes. All she had to do was say yes, and he would open her eyes to the most beautiful thing two tortured souls could share.

Her eyes fell to the floor, and just like that, their connection was lost. Her rejection stung more than it had any other time before. He needed to get away from her.

"It was nice meeting you, Shayna King."

Greg held her hand and lifted it to his mouth, kissing her palm gently. Shayna watched as he walked to the door and prayed he wasn't walking out of her life forever.

"Greg?"

He turned to her but didn't speak.

"Be patient with me. I'm learning how to be happy all over again."

"I don't think you're truly allowing yourself to do that, Shayna."

CHAPTER 26

"Surprise!" The room erupted as Greg stepped into Gavin's house. He surveyed the room to see Gavin and his former fiancée, Amya, Troy, Drake, Ryan, and little Chyna standing in the middle of the room saluting him. After calling things off with Molina, Gavin and Amya had rekindled their relationship for the sake of Chyna.

"What is going on here?"

Greg walked over to Chyna and picked her up. He walked around the room, hugging each guest.

"It's a going away party, brother," Gavin said as they embraced.

"Carmen sends her love. You know we are at the finish line."

"I'm sorry I'm going to miss it. Send me lots of pictures, man," he said to Troy.

"No doubt."

"Well, I thank you all for coming out to see me off," he said as he hugged the last guest.

"Don't forget about me. I came all the way back to make sure you made your flight."

Greg turned to see Arie entering and couldn't stop the smile that touched his lips. She was more excited than he was about the move.

"Oh, ye of little faith."

"I didn't become successful taking chances. I would like to formally introduce you to my assistant, Krissy. You two have talked back and forth, so it's time for an official introduction.

"Nice to finally meet you, Krissy."

"Same here. Arie can't stop raving about you, so I'm definitely glad we have you on board."

Greg eyed the very petite fair-skinned beauty as she smiled at him. She held out her hand to him, and he took it in his.

"I have another guest who wanted to come and show you love."

The petite Puerto Rican beauty poked her head in the door before completely stepping in. Her big radiant smile caused Greg to smile as she pounced on him.

"Papi, you are looking good, my friend," Nikki said as Greg held her tightly.

Nikki was Arie's best friend since college and the maid of honor at their wedding, even though they'd eloped. She was a loyal friend and fan of Greg and Arie.

"So do you. How have you been?"

"I cannot complain. Life has been good. What about my girl right here?" she asked, twirling Arie around. "Aren't you so proud of her?"

"I most certainly am." Greg pulled Arie into an embrace.

"It's good to see you two back together again. It hurt my soul when you guys split up. My girl was so upset. She still hasn't managed to find a man to fill your shoes."

Greg eyed Arie suspiciously. Nikki's statement confused him. Arie had been the one to call off their marriage and walk away from him.

"Nikki, baby, let me introduce you to everyone," Arie said, pulling her away from Greg who followed them.

"I'll make the introductions," Greg said, noticing Ryan eyeing Arie.

Arie was impeccably dressed as always, leaving little to the imagination in the skin-tight pencil dress she wore.

"Of course, you know Gavin."

Arie hugged him tightly.

"I missed you, brother-in-law."

"Same here. I'm so proud of you, young lady."

"That means a lot coming from you, Mr. Big Shot."

Arie grabbed Nikki's hand.

"You remember Nikki, right?"

"Yes, it's been a while. How are you, Nikki?"

"Gavin, nice to see you again," Nikki responded.

"I'd like to introduce you to Amya, and our daughter, Chyna."

"Hello, Amya and Chyna," Arie and Nikki said, grabbing their hands.

"I love your work, Arie."

"Oh, thank you, Amya."

"I'm going to take this little one and put her to bed. Greg, congratulations again," she said, kissing him on the cheek.

"Over here, you remember Ryan and Drake?"

Both gentlemen shook Nikki and Arie's hand. Ryan held on to Arie a little longer than Drake.

"How are you, Arie? It's been years."

"Yes, and you still look the same."

"I'll take that. You, on the other hand, look better than ever."

Greg stood between the two of them. "Enough already."

"Man, she's your ex-wife. You can't still claim her!" Ryan yelled across the room, as Greg pulled her away from him.

Gavin and Drake laughed at the exchange.

"I don't know. It looks like those two are heading for a reunion," Nikki added.

"It's time to toast the occasion!" Arie yelled, ignoring Nikki's statement.

Gavin appeared with a tray of champagne glasses and passed them around the room. Arie grabbed Greg and pulled him into her arms.

"I'm so excited about our next chapter. I know we are about to create greatness, and I look forward to the journey."

"Here, here!" Nikki yelled, holding up her glass.

Shayna watched from the door as Arie and Greg embraced. She hated how perfect they looked together and how Greg looked at Arie like she was pure perfection. She listened quietly as Arie spoke about their reunion, and she felt a sense of jealousy at the way he looked so happy without her. She wished she could be what Greg deserved.

"Shayna, come in."

Gavin ushered Shayna into the house, and Greg released Arie when he noticed her. Like always, she did a little something to his soul every time he saw her. She was definitely dressed to leave an impression on his heart. The fitted bodysuit fit like a glove, and her curls were still untamed just like she wore it on their date. He noticed she wore the earrings he'd purchased for her as well.

"Come here," he said, pulling her into an embrace. "I'm glad you could make it."

"I wouldn't be anywhere else. This house is amazing."

"Yeah, I guess my parents were right about the whole surgeon thing after all."

Shayna smiled at him.

"Shayna, girl, you look amazing," Arie said, joining them.

"I'd like to introduce you to my good friend, Nikki."

"Hi, Nikki."

"Now, can I get my hands on Arie?" Ryan yelled, causing laughter to erupt from everyone.

"In your dreams, little man," Arie responded.

"Shayna? Shayna King?"

The foursome turned at the sound of a small voice calling Shayna's name. She looked into familiar eyes as Krissy looked back at her.

"What are you doing here?" she asked. Shayna looked panic stricken. She didn't respond as Krissy continuously asked what she was doing there.

"Krissy?" Arie touched her arm.

"You don't understand, Arie. You don't know who this woman is."

Greg stood in front of Shayna protectively.

"What's going on here, Arie?"

"I don't know."

"Shayna?"

"Tell them who I am. Tell them how because of you my brother is dead. Tell them what a selfish bitch you are, Shayna King." Krissy read off her allegations so calmly. It was scary.

"Krissy, I think you have the wrong person." Greg turned his attention to Shayna.

"What is she talking about?" He was confused. It was obvious Shayna knew Krissy, so why wasn't she defending herself against the lies?

"Let's go, Krissy," Arie said, pulling her toward the door with Nikki's assistance.

"She knows the truth!" she yelled over her shoulder at Shayna as Arie escorted her out.

Gavin ushered everyone out of the room, giving them privacy. Greg turned to her once he knew they were alone. Shayna's eyes held those same damn tears that never seemed to fall. He wanted answers. Why had this stranger just accused her of being the cause of her brother's death? Things were starting to make sense, yet he still had so many unanswered questions, and the person who held the answers was standing before him with no explanation.

"What is she talking about, Shayna?"

Shayna threw her hands up at him and charged toward the door. Greg blocked the entrance, not allowing her to leave. She owed him an explanation, and he was damn sure going to get it.

"Talk to me, Shayna."

"I can't!"

"You can't keep running away from me."

"What do you want me to say, Greg? She's right! I'm responsible for her brother's death."

Her words caused Greg to tense, and he moved out of her way. Shayna pushed past him and fled at top speed. Greg had no desire to follow her.

CHAPTER 27

*G*reg sat in his office on the 22nd floor, overlooking Downtown Manhattan. The building housed *Black Excellence Magazine,* along with three other major companies, including his and Troy's second studio. Navarro and Black Photography had two locations. This particular location was prime real estate in Manhattan that had come as part of his proposal from Arie. Troy had been delighted with the idea of a Manhattan location, and he had to admit the pride his parents had shown made him feel good. He'd long since stopped trying to please his parents, but it definitely warmed him that his mother was so proud. The only downfall to the job was leaving at a time he felt his brother needed him the most.

While having Chyna in his life had softened Gavin, what his parents and Amya had done had hardened him. The longing he still had for Molina was evident, and Greg wished there was something he could do to help his brother. Greg allowed his thoughts to rest on Shayna. The move certainly had pulled them even further apart, and Greg felt the distance was good for them.

Krissy was asked to take some time off after her verbal attack on Shayna. Arie had insisted Krissy had never shown that side of her and was an amazing assistant. For that reason, she hadn't been let go, and

Greg agreed with the decision. Greg initially wanted to ask Krissy about what happened with Shayna but thought better of it. He needed to hear it from Shayna. He wanted her to trust him enough to share her secrets just as she'd shared her body. Shayna hadn't done that. Instead, she'd left him to wonder without any explanation.

"Knock, knock."

Arie's temporary assistant peeked in her head at him. The voluptuous red head was smiling as usual as her wavy hair flowed around her face.

"Hey, Amber."

"Arie is back in the office, and she wanted to see you."

"Let her know I'll be there in a sec."

"Sure thing."

Amber left the office, closing the door softly behind her. Arie had been traveling and out of the office for most of the time he'd been in New York. Greg picked up the portfolio filled with pictures for the next layout and headed toward her office.

"Hey, you," Arie said as Greg entered her office. Arie held the biggest most luxurious office he'd ever seen. The corner office held the best view of Manhattan with its massive floor to ceiling windows. Arie sat behind a large glass desk she kept meticulously neat. She had framed covers lined neatly on her walls and a photo he'd taken very early in his career. Greg had been flattered when he saw she owned it. He remembered the piece, a skyline shot of San Diego, had sold for top dollar, and he finally knew why. Arie had told him it reminded her of home, not just the city but the feel of being married to him.

"Well, look who decided to come to work today?"

"Even when I'm not here, I'm working."

"You should really consider taking some time off. I haven't seen you relax since I've been here, not even weekends."

"Those are the breaks when you run your own empire."

Arie looked at him before she started talking again.

"I'm so glad to have you here, Greg. I love my staff and the people I work with, but it doesn't compare to having someone here I know has my back. I really hope you like living in Manhattan," she said, leaving the comment lingering in the air.

Greg loved being in Manhattan and enjoyed the culture, but he had to admit, he missed home. He missed being with his family and meeting his niece. Having to leave was killing him. Even still, he had no plans to move back. Not having to be near or see Shayna was the solace he found whenever he longed for home.

"I miss my family from time to time, but for the most part, New York has been good to me. You've done a wonderful job making sure I feel at home, so thank you."

"How are your living arrangements?"

"Tight compared to the space I had in San Diego, but I like it."

"I'm glad."

Greg took a seat in the empty chair in front of her desk and placed his portfolio on top of it, sliding it to her.

"Thank you. I'll look through them later tonight."

"Why don't you wait to do that, and let's go out tonight?"

Arie glanced up at him suspiciously, locking gazes with him. "Are you asking me on a date, Mr. Navarro?"

Greg chuckled.

"As friends. I need to get you away from this office. Allow yourself to let your hair down and show me the Arie I used to know. Come on. It'll be fun."

"OK, let's do it."

GREG PULLED out a sports jacket from his closet to add to his look of fitted jeans and a crisp white T-shirt. He wore a pair of caramel colored loafers made for walking as he planned to do a lot of that with Arie. He looked forward to their evening together as he remembered the night of her dad's birthday. They'd had so much fun together reminiscing, laughing at each other's corny jokes, and even sitting in comfortable silence together. That night was also the night he'd slept with Shayna for the first and only time. It was the one time she'd let herself need him. She made him feel like he was the only man that could fulfill her need at the time. Greg heard Arie knock at the door, and he shrugged into his jacket. That woman always insisted they take that damn limousine everywhere. He chuckled to himself as he grabbed his keys and rushed to the door.

"I hope you have on walking shoes because we're going to do some walking today, little woman."

"Does it look like I dressed for walking, sir?" she asked as he swung the door open.

Greg glanced down at the heels she wore with skinny jeans and an off the shoulder floral top. The heels had to be six inches, yet he still towered over her.

"Do you own anything other than heels?"

"I have a pair of sneakers I wear for running, but I can't wear those on a date."

Greg laughed out loud.

"Of course not. Let's get out of here."

Greg ushered her out of the door and to the car where the driver was waiting with the door open for them. Arie slid in as Greg whispered something to the driver before joining her.

"What was that about?"

"Relax, and don't worry about it."

Arie sat back in her seat and smiled at him. Relinquishing control was not something she was used to doing, but with Greg, she was completely comfortable.

They sat in silence as the driver drove to their destination. Thirty minutes later, the car stopped in front of the mall. Arie gave Greg a quizzical look as he opened the door, preparing to get out.

"I'll be right back," he said, hopping out of the car and jogging into the mall.

Arie waited impatiently for Greg to return, scrolling through her phone to keep her mind off of the wait.

When he returned, he slid back into the car holding one single bag and a smile that made her laugh.

"Greg Navarro, what are you up too?"

Greg placed her feet into his lap, removing both heels before removing a pair of pink and gold Nike running shoes out of his bag. He placed newly purchased socks on her feet before lacing her shoes and placing them over the socks.

"You remembered what size shoe I wear?"

"You were my wife, Arie. Of course I remember."

"These are adorable, but why do I need running shoes?"

"Because we're ditching this damn limousine, and we are going to be New York tourists for the evening. I even brought my camera to capture the moment."

"No, Greg. I can't."

"You can, and you will."

They pulled up to Central Park, and Greg helped Arie out of the car. She looked down at her newly purchased sneakers and laughed. The fact they were fashionable and matched her top did help just a little.

"I have never been to Central Park, so I thought we could explore it together. I know it's cheesy and a little touristy for a vet like yourself, but I was hoping you'd do this with me."

"Don't judge me, but I've never actually been here either."

Greg shook his head.

"That does not surprise me because you're a workaholic. It'll be a first for both of us. How about we start with a bike ride?"

"I haven't ridden a bike in forever!"

Greg grabbed her hand, and they ran to the bike rental stand. He paid for two bikes, jumping on one, and started riding down the nearest trail. Arie squealed as she tried getting acclimated with the bike. Greg snapped pictures of her as he circled around her, and she sped up, trying to pass him, laughing all the while. They rode for miles, enjoying the scenery and stopping to take pictures here and there before they came to the Belvedere Castle. They both stopped to marvel at it as the sun began to set behind it, giving the castle an orange halo.

"How beautiful is that?"

Greg pulled out his camera and began snapping pictures. He let the bike drop to the ground as he got closer.

"Come over here."

Arie let her bike fall to the ground as well and stood next to him. Greg grabbed her hand and placed her in front of the view of the castle and began snapping shots of her.

"What are you doing?"

"Just be natural."

"How can I be natural when you have a camera in my face?"

"Just find a spot on the building to look at, and focus on it."

Arie did as she was told as Greg snapped photo after photo of her. Her impatience kicked in, and she started forcing poses. She lifted her pant leg, showing off her new shoes and proceeded to make funny faces as Greg continued snapping and egging her on.

He loved how she brought out the kid in him and vice versa. She appeared to be having a great time, and his camera didn't lie.

"Come on. Let's grab something to eat and relax a bit."

They walked their bikes to the nearest bike rental stand before grabbing a couple of hotdogs at a nearby vendor and took a seat on a park bench.

"That was actually a lot of fun," Arie said, taking a bite of her hotdog.

"I told you it would be. You don't have to always go high maintenance to have a good time."

"I think I forgot about that. When you've struggled most of your life and don't have to anymore, you forget about the little things that used to make you happy. I'm so glad I have you here to remind me. You always knew how to bring me back to the real me."

Arie grabbed his hand, and they linked fingers. Greg felt that same feeling of home as she held tighter. He wondered what she was feeling. He didn't want to misread her a second time, but he was getting that vibe.

"Either that was the best hotdog ever, or I was starving."

"I'd have to agree it was pretty amazing. Let's get out of here. What do you say we go visit the Statue of Liberty next?"

"I've never been there either," she said, covering her face in mock shame.

"Well, tonight, we're covering all the stops."

"Let's do it!"

When they reached Greg's brownstone, they ate New York style deep dish pizza and opened the bottle of wine they'd purchased on the way. Arie sat atop the kitchen counter as Greg washed the dishes following dinner. He glanced over at her as she swung her feet, looking almost childlike.

"You told me you haven't dated a man since we divorced. Why is that?"

"I think you and I both know the answer."

"The last time I assumed something about us, I made a complete ass of myself. Why don't you save me the embarrassment and just tell me?"

Arie stopped swinging her feet and placed both hands on either side of her.

"Do you really want to have this conversation? It may get a little deeper than you are ready for."

Greg dried the last dish and placed it in the cabinet before giving Arie his full attention. He stood in front of her, leaning back on the refrigerator.

"I could use some good, honest, adult conversation."

Arie cleared her throat before beginning.

"I know I said I wasn't interested in starting things over with you, but that wasn't entirely true. Even though I was the one who called it quits on the marriage, I never stopped being in love with you."

Greg's heart pounded in his chest hearing Arie's confessions of love for him.

"I knew we needed to be apart to find out who we were individually, but I always thought we would find our way back. We started off as great friends, but it was too hard just being friends with the person you wanted to spend forever with."

"Why didn't you ever say anything?"

"Because I'm the one who asked for a divorce. I knew I couldn't just come back into your life and say 'hey, you know that divorce I wanted? Well, never mind.'"

"I'm sorry. I didn't know. I just thought you were busy building your empire and didn't have time to feed into our friendship."

Arie shook her head. "No, you are and will always be my best friend, Greg."

Greg approached her, placing his hands on each side of her.

"Same here."

Arie leaned in and kissed him. Greg's full lips covered her mouth. Arie wrapped her hands around his neck and spread her legs so that Greg could get closer. He rested lazily between her legs as they continued to explore one another with their mouths.

"I could get used to doing this again," she whispered once their mouths parted.

Greg chuckled. While he enjoyed their kiss, he didn't want to lead her on. He was still unsure where he stood with Shayna and didn't want to bring Arie into his life, adding to his confusion.

"What was that about?"

"I forgot what it was like to kiss you."

"And you just all of a sudden needed a reminder?" he teased.

"Yeah. I had a wonderful day with you, and I'm not looking forward to ending it."

Greg moved away from her so he could look into her eyes. It was time for them to discuss what was happening between them.

"Arie, we have to be really careful with this. You mean too much to me to allow anything to destroy our friendship."

"And you think us trying again will destroy us?"

"I'm not saying that."

"What are you saying?"

"I'm saying I don't want to hurt you."

"Because you're in love with Shayna?"

Greg walked away, and Arie hopped off the counter to follow him. He took a seat on the couch, leaving enough space for Arie to take a seat.

"You can say it. I'm a big girl."

"I honestly don't know what my feelings are for her, but what I'm one hundred percent sure of is how much I care about you. You will always be a part of my life."

"So, why don't we explore that part and see what happens?" she asked.

"Because I don't want to lose you again if it doesn't work out."

"You won't. I pinky promise." Arie held out her pinky to him, and Greg wrapped his pinky around hers. She laid her head on his shoulder, and they sat in silence, both contemplating what was to come of restarting their relationship.

ARIE MADE her way down the hallway of Greg's brownstone after showering and slipping into one of his shirts. Greg had slipped into the shower as she exited just like old times, and Arie smiled at the memory of them. She rummaged through the refrigerator to see what he had that she could fix them for breakfast, deciding on spinach and tomato omelets. Their evening had ended much like their day, with Arie feeling a sense of belonging with Greg. They'd talked well into the night about the what if's of starting over until they both fell asleep in each other's arms. They hadn't solidified their relationship, but Arie was sure they would discuss it over breakfast. She placed two plates on the table and slid a steaming omelet on each, placing a protein smoothie next to his and water next to her plate.

Greg smelled the aroma of the breakfast as he exited the shower, dried off, and threw on his running shorts. His mouth was watering at the thought of the delicious meal he was sure Arie prepared for him. She was a great cook but couldn't imagine what she'd come up with using what little he held in his refrigerator. He pulled the shirt over his head while stepping out of his room.

"Whatever you're cooking smells amazing."

Greg's words went missing as his eyes rested on Shayna who stood next to Arie. They both looked at him, waiting to see his reaction.

"Shayna?" He said her name like a question as if he didn't know if it were truly her. Was he hallucinating, or was Shayna King standing in his home all the way in Manhattan?

"I'm sorry. I didn't know you had company."

Greg's anger hit before any other emotion, and he was sure his face displayed it. He was angry with himself because the sight of her still did something to him. He wanted to hate her and to have her out of his system. Her timing couldn't be worse as he saw Arie standing next to her in nothing but his shirt.

"Is everyone OK? Is something wrong with my family or yours?"

Shayna looked at him with a puzzled expression.

"Oh no. Everyone is fine."

"So, what's up, Shayna?" he asked, pulling his shirt down over his abdomen.

Shayna toyed with her hands, and Greg could see she was searching for the right words. The truth was the only thing he wanted from her at the moment.

"I'm going to give you two some privacy," Arie said, making a hasty retreat to his room.

Greg noticed Shayna watch Arie enter his bedroom and shut the door. He could see the hurt in her eyes, but why? It was her decision they keep things platonic.

The room was much too small to hold the emotions the two of them held. He felt like he was suffocating as he pointed her in the direction of the living room. Shayna obliged, entering the living room and taking a seat. Greg sat in the chair across from her, insuring he was not too close.

"What brings you to New York?"

"I needed to talk to you."

"And you couldn't' just call me?"

"This couldn't be said over the phone. I felt you deserved to hear it from me in person."

"I'm listening." His tone let her know he had no desire to pick up playing the guessing game they'd played for far too long.

"This is what I tried to prevent from happening between us. I knew my secrets were too heavy for you or anyone else to handle for that matter."

"How would you know? You never gave me the opportunity to be there for you. You just convinced yourself I wouldn't."

"You didn't fight for me to stay once you heard Krissy's accusations."

"Fight for you? That's all I've been doing since I've met you, Shayna. I should have heard it from you first, and maybe I wouldn't have been caught off guard. I know you're not a monster. I'm sure there's more to the story than what Krissy said in the heat of the moment. Why don't you for once tell me what's going on with you, Shayna?"

Shayna lowered her eyes and took a deep breath.

"The guy in the picture you asked me about was my fiancé and Krissy's brother. He's the guy I told you about before."

"Shawn?" he asked, remembering the name she'd said in her sleep.

"Yes."

Greg sat quietly. She was finally about to tell him her truth, what she'd been holding back from him all of these months.

"We were young and in love. We had big dreams and planned out this fabulous life together. A few months after we were engaged is when I lost my parents. They were driving home from a weekend getaway my father planned and were hit by a drunk driver. They both died instantly." Shayna's voice cracked just a little, and Greg wanted to reach out to her but thought better of it.

"Shawn tried helping me through the grieving stage, but grief is a funny thing. I was reckless in my grief. I didn't want to love, because I knew with love came loss, and loss is devastating. So, I pushed him away, and he continued to fight for us. One night, he called and asked if he could take me out, and I told him I was too busy."

Shayna paused a deep heavy pause as her eyes held unshed tears.

"He made plans to go out with his friends. When he returned home, he was shot only a few feet from his door. The case went unsolved, and his family blames me."

"That wasn't your fault, Shayna," Greg said, unable to stop himself.

It was obvious Shawn's family wasn't the only ones to blame her; she blamed herself.

"I was with another guy that night," she blurted out. Greg could sense the hurt and guilt she held, but like always, she didn't release it.

"I turned him down to be with someone else, and he was murdered. If only I'd been there for him, maybe he would still be here."

There it was. The reason she'd built a wall so tall and so heavy no one could break it down. She held so much guilt she didn't want anyone to break it. She wanted to wallow in her pain because she thought she deserved it.

"You don't know that. You could have been with him, Shayna, and then what, huh? What if you'd decided to be with him and both of you were there that night? Do you think he would have wanted that?"

"Of course not."

"No one can say what would have happened. That's not rational thinking, sweetheart."

"Grief isn't rational sometimes, Greg." She looked at him with sad eyes.

"I felt you should know why I couldn't let you love me. Like I said before, I'm not easy, Greg. The night you came home and I was having the nightmare, that was only one of many I've had. I'd just learned Shawn's case was being reopened, and with it, all my old wounds reopened as well. Not only for me but for his family. Hence, Krissy's reaction to me."

"That was just her pain talking."

"It doesn't make it any less painful for me or them. I'm sorry you got dragged into my mess, but lucky for us, you found out before we became anything to each other."

Greg watched her struggle with her emotions.

"It's too late, Shayna. We did become something to each other."

"I never wanted to hurt you, Greg. That is why I jumped on a plane to come here to talk to you. You mean enough to me that I had to let you know everything so that you can move on... maybe even with Arie."

Greg flinched when she said her name. He'd forgotten she was still there.

Arie stepped into the living room, fully dressed with her shoes in her hand.

"My driver's here. I'm going to go. Call me later, Greg." Greg noticed she avoided looking him in the eyes. He glanced at the table and the breakfast she'd taken time out to fix him and felt guilt rush over him.

"Arie, I'm sorry," he said as he stood to walk her to the door. He wrapped his arms around her and placed a kiss on her forehead.

"Call me later," she said before walking out of the door. When she was gone, Greg felt the anger he felt toward Shayna creep back into place. While he was glad she finally shared her secrets with him, it angered him she waited this long to trust him.

"Again, I'm sorry for interrupting. I just thought you deserved to hear all of this from me. I couldn't live with myself if you thought it was because of you we couldn't work out."

"But you let me carry that load for this entire time, Shayna," he spat.

"I didn't know how to tell you."

"Like you just did! I have been begging you to let me in, to let me help you, and you wait until I move to another state to hop on a plane and come and tell me this?"

"I thought this was what you wanted?"

"No, it's not what I wanted, Shayna. I wanted you to tell me before it got to this point. You didn't do this for me. You did this for yourself."

Shayna stood abruptly.

"Of course, I did it for you. I was perfectly fine before you came into my life!"

"No, you were a coward before I came into your life!" Greg knew his words were harsh, but they were also the truth, and the truth hurt sometimes.

"I gave you something worth fighting for, and you threw it back in my face."

"That's not fair, Greg."

"But it's true."

"Maybe you did give me something to fight for, but I don't have any fight in me."

"We know you're not a fighter. You walk out on the thought of being happy."

Those words hit Shayna like a ton of bricks, knocking the wind out of her. She hadn't expected Greg to be so short and angry with her, but his verbal attacks were hitting like daggers to her already damaged heart.

"I guess that's my queue to leave."

"I guess it is."

Shayna walked slowly to the door, looking back at Greg only for a brief second before reaching the door.

"I wish you and Arie the best."

CHAPTER 28

*S*hayna busied herself at the café, stocking the supply closet with things she didn't really need, but she had to keep moving in order to keep her mind occupied on anything but Greg. She was still struggling with sleep, but now, her nightmares were about Greg, and it confused and hurt Shayna at the same time. Instead of watching Shawn get shot when he turned to her, it was Greg's face she saw. She felt like she'd lost him too. The way he'd spoken to her, calling her a coward, saying she wasn't a fighter had truly hurt. What hurt the most was she knew he was telling the truth; she was a coward, and she was scared to love again. The thoughts of he and Arie starting over invaded her mind during the day, and she could not stop thinking about her standing next to him in nothing but his shirt. She wondered if they'd made love the night before. Had he done those same things to Arie's body that he'd done to her the night they'd made love for the first time? She had every intention on confessing her love for him and asking if he'd be willing to take things slow with her and figure it out. When Arie answered the door, she knew she was too late. She knew she couldn't hurt him anymore by confessing her love for him, so instead, she just gave him her truth. She hadn't expected him to be so angry with her, but his words had delivered an ugly hurtful truth.

She'd also looked up Krissy while in New York with the help of Arie. She reached out to her, and Krissy had agreed to have lunch with her before she was scheduled to fly back to San Diego. Their meeting started out full of tension, but Shayna did apologize to Krissy for not being there for her brother, which eased things just a little. She explained to her the space she'd been in after losing her parents, and Krissy seemed to understand just a little more. Krissy apologized for attacking Shayna, explaining the case being reopened had her sensitive, much like it had with Shayna. They'd left not as friends but with a better understanding of the other, and Shayna hoped it brought Krissy just a little bit of peace the way it had with her.

"You're going to run out of room in there."

Shayna turned to see the ever-fashionable Q approaching the area she was working in.

"Hey, Q. What are you doing here?"

"I came to check on my friend. I haven't talk to you in quite some time now."

Shayna had avoided her friend and tried avoiding her sisters since returning from New York. Carmen and Molina hadn't been so easy to avoid, but she hadn't talked to Q in weeks. She didn't want any of them to know what a fool she'd made of herself in New York, but her sisters had forced it out of her. Carmen was due to deliver any day. It was a welcome distraction from Shayna's complicated life.

"I heard they finally arrested the guy who shot Shawn. Do you want to talk about it?"

"There's not really much to talk about. The fact that it was just so random, and the guy tried to rob him doesn't make sense. He lost his life over something so senseless."

Q sat her bag down on the counter and walked into the supply closet with Shayna.

"Yeah, you almost want it to be something more just so it can make sense."

"Exactly!"

"I hear ya. Well, how did it go in New York?"

Shayna began placing things back in the supply closet again.

"Well, I'm here alone, and he's there reunited with his ex-wife. I messed up, and I really don't want to think or talk about it because it hurts too damn much."

Q threw her hands in the air and backed out of the closet.

"I'm sorry. I just wanted to help."

Shayna stopped placing items in the closet and turned to Q.

"I'm sorry. I didn't mean to snap."

"I know you didn't."

"I really just want and need to put all of this behind me. Shawn's murder has been solved, and now, he can rest. Greg is building a new life with Arie, and I think it's great if he's happy."

"Do you think he's happy?"

"Yeah, I do. The way they look at each other... there's no denying they still care for one another."

"You know I don't think I've ever heard you say how you really feel about Greg. How do you feel about Greg, Shayna? Say it out loud so at least you can hear it, even if he can't."

"That sounds silly."

"Maybe, but it might make you feel a little better."

Shayna closed her eyes.

"I love him, Q. I'm in love with him. Why do I lose everyone I love?"

"Shayna, I'm sorry," she said, wrapping her arms around her.

"I think you should tell Greg how you feel. Allow yourself to be vulnerable with him. Shayna, he's done that for you, and who knows? Maybe he feels the same way about you."

"I couldn't do that to Arie. I happen to like her."

"You can still like her, but all is fair in love and war. Now we just have to figure out a way to get your man."

CHAPTER 29

$\mathcal{A}$rie scrolled through photo after photo of pictures from Greg's last session, trying to select a photo for *Black Excellence* next cover. Each photo brought a different flare, and Arie was having a hard time trying to narrow it down to just one. Greg was so talented and always brought something fresh to the table. Arie loved it although it made her job harder.

"Krissy, is Greg in office yet?"

"He actually just walked in. Do you want me to have him come to your office?"

"No, I will go to him."

Arie picked up her iPad and headed to Greg's office, which wasn't too far from her own. She tapped on the door before walking in and found Greg powering on his own iPad.

"Hey, are you busy?"

"Hey, I just got in. I've been working in the studio all morning on a private photoshoot. Come on in, and have a seat.

"How's the studio doing?"

"It's starting to pick up. There's a lot of opportunity here for us to grow, and I'm excited about it."

"That's amazing. I have been going through the cover photos you submitted, and I'm stumped. They're all so good. You are too good at your job."

"Well, let's take a look at them, and you give me a little more information on the concept. Let's see if we can't narrow it down to one.

"OK." Arie powered on her iPad and pulled up the covers. "So, this issue we are focusing on the natural hair movement, right?"

Greg nodded as she continued.

"So, we have this amazing shot of Solange with this beautiful full afro. We have Lupita with her short, sassy curls and glowing, dark skin. She's the face of black girl magic right now, and the new 'it' girl, coming off the success of *Black Panther*. Then the ever classy and classic Jilly from Philly with the locs and whose smile would have those bad boys rolling off the stands. You throw in this one of Carmen. This woman's hair is beyond gorgeous, and this photo is breathtaking. How do I choose just one!"

"I know. I added the last one of Carmen because I felt like using a non-celebrity would be appealing to the readers. Troy actually shot the one of Carmen. When I think natural hair movement, she was the first person that came to mind. Carmen just has something that appeals to everyone."

"I know what you mean. She's radiant."

"I have two suggestions if you just can't choose. I can edit the photos and combine them all onto one cover, or you can have a multi-cover issue this month. Let the readers decide which one they want."

Arie eyed him with a little sparkle in her eye.

"You are a genius! I love the idea of a multi-cover issue!"

"Well there you go. Problem solved."

Arie picked up the photo of Carmen.

"How are Carmen and Troy doing? I know they are excited about being new parents."

"Yeah, they are. Troy Jr. is doing well. I plan to visit next week so I can meet the new addition."

"Do you plan to see Shayna while you're there?"

"I'm sure I'm bound to run into her."

"How do you feel about seeing her again? I know you guys didn't end the last visit on a positive note."

"I don't know. I guess I'll cross that bridge when I get to it."

Arie placed the photo back on his desk and stood up.

"Look, Greg. You know I'm a straight shooter most of the time. I've noticed a change in you since Shayna's visit, and I understand you've had mixed feelings about her, but I thought you and I were working toward something. That all just stopped without any explanation from you, and it's been weeks. Don't you think I deserve an explanation?"

She was right, of course. Greg hadn't brought up their date or night together since Shayna's visit. He'd simply sent her a text apologizing a second time. Shayna had left his mind spinning after she'd told him about Shawn and her parents. She suffered a great deal of loss, but as much as Greg wanted to be there for her, he wasn't ready to be pushed away yet again. Arie deserved so much more from him. He hated disappointing her, but appeared he'd done just that.

"You do," he said, standing and walking around the desk. "I'm sorry you had to ask me for an explanation when I should have given it to you. Our time together was great. Being with you is like being home; you provide me with so much peace. We know the real about each other. I can be myself with you. We laugh together, and you've been one of my biggest supporters."

"Same here," she whispered.

"You are my best friend, Arie."

"If we're all of that to each other, why can't we seem to make this work?"

"Honestly, because my heart is with Shayna. Although she's complicated, tough, and not at all easy, I'm in love with her. I'm sorry, Arie.

Arie allowed her head to fall as a tear escaped. Greg stepped to her and brushed the fallen tear from her face.

"I could be with you and be perfectly content and happy, but you deserve so much more."

"Thank you for being honest." She smiled at him, and Greg pulled her into his arms.

"Greg."

"Yeah?"

"You're fired."

Greg pulled away and looked down at Arie to see she was serious.

"Go home, and get your girl."

CHAPTER 30

Shayna opened the door of her condo, taking her shoes off at the door. She placed the bag she was carrying on the counter and flipped through the mail she'd retrieved from the mail box.

"Men have it way too easy."

Startled, Shayna dropped the mail to the floor at the sound of Greg's voice. She looked up to see him sitting comfortably on her couch, toying with the camera he held in his hand.

"Sorry, I didn't mean to startle you. Molina gave me her key to get in. I hope you don't mind."

She scrambled to retrieve the mail, and Greg placed his camera to the side and knelt down to help her. They stood at the same time, both holding on to the piece of paper for dear life.

"What are you doing here?"

"I came to see the baby and to see you."

Shayna took the paper from his hand and walked to the kitchen, placing it on the counter. She needed to do something with her hands to distract herself. She didn't want hope to creep into her mind too soon.

"I'm not done fighting, Shayna."

Shayna closed her eyes, keeping her back to him.

"What about your job?"

"Arie fired me."

Shayna whirled around to see if he was serious. He stood staring at her, and she could see in his eyes he was telling the truth.

"Why would she do that when she fought so hard to get you there?"

Greg walked toward her and took her hands into his.

"Because Arie is an amazing woman and friend. She knew my heart wasn't in New York."

Shayna pulled her hands from his and walked back to the living room. She could feel Greg following behind her. He stopped her, forcing Shayna to turn around and look at him.

"Shayna, this is it, baby. This is all the fight I have left in me. You asked me to be patient with you, and I've done that." He touched her hair then her face before stepping away from her.

"Just tell me what I can do?"

She looked at him through her tears. It was the first time he'd actually seen her cry, and it saddened him that it hurt her to love him back.

"Can you bring him back? Just so I can tell him I'm sorry. Can you bring my parents back so that I can have one last conversation with them?"

Greg shook his head.

"No, I can't bring them back, sweetheart, but I can hold you until you are yourself and then fall in love with you all over again."

She smiled just a bit through her tears.

"That's fictional, Greg."

"I'm right here telling you it's not. The way I feel for you is far from fiction, baby. All you have to do is say yes."

Shayna didn't say anything, although her heart tried to force her to scream "yes." Everything she wanted was standing in front of her with pleading eyes, but the love she had for him wouldn't let her speak. Greg deserved so much more than her brokenness. Wasn't love sacrifice? If she truly loved him as much as her heart was screaming, shouldn't she let him go so he could have a life greater than what she could give to him?

With her silence came Greg's defeat as his eyes fell to the floor. He grabbed his camera and placed her key on the table before turning his back to her. Greg reached the door, placing his hand and the door-knob just as Shayna spoke.

"I wasn't supposed to love anybody else. My love was supposed to be just for him, but I failed and gave my heart to you without even realizing it."

Greg turned to see her tear stained face. She held her hands in a praying position close to her mouth, and for a moment, he wondered if she was doing just that.

"He was everything to me, and still, I love you more," she whispered.

Greg watched her as all of the pain, guilt, and fear came pouring out with her tears. Her cries where gut-wrenching, and Greg rushed to her, dropping his camera to the floor as he pulled her into his arms. She melted into him and sobbed so hard it brought tears to his own eyes.

Shayna tried pushing him away, but Greg refused to let her go this time. He had never witnessed this much pain in anyone, and he never wanted to again. Shayna was completely falling apart in front of him. Greg lifted her into his arms so that she wouldn't hit the floor. He stood holding her, rocking her back and forth like a baby doing what he could to sooth her. He held her like that until her cries turned to whimpers. He walked her to the bedroom, laying her gently in the bed before climbing in next to her. They stayed like that until her whim-pers turned to heavy breathing, and Greg knew that she was sleep. He stroked her hair while watching her sleep, wishing he could remove the pain that she'd just exposed to him. He just wanted to hold her if only for the night. He wanted to ease her fears.

SHAYNA OPENED her heavy eyelids to find Greg asleep next to her. He was still fully clothed, not even his shoes were missing, and he held her so tight she wasn't sure how she was able to breathe. She felt safe and warm in his arms, and the thought of moving caused a shiver to overcome her. Shayna placed a hand to his face and felt the stubble breaking through his smooth skin. The sunlight began to peek through the window, telling her that morning had found them, and Shayna delighted in the way the sun danced around his face. Greg had turned out to be her hero, the man that she loved and who had stolen her heart, even when it wasn't hers to give. The love she had for Shawn and the guilt from the way he was taken had her heart on lock, yet Greg had found the key. He'd brought her love that she never thought that she would discover. Shayna didn't feel deserving, but there she was—in the moment with him, and he loved her.

"What are you doing?" Greg asked, catching Shayna staring at him.

Shayna smiled at him while stroking his face. Greg returned the smile and tightened his hold on her.

"I was just thinking how wonderful you are."

"Oh yeah?"

"Yeah," she answered, nodding her head. "Thank you for not giving up on me."

"Thank you for letting me in."

"I'm sorry I couldn't do that before now."

"Now is all that matters."

"I know I look a mess right now," she said, placing a hand over her face.

"A beautiful mess," he said removing her hand.

Greg shifted and propped his head up on his elbow so that he could look her in the eyes. Shayna enjoyed the view his shift allowed her.

"What happened with you and Arie? I could tell that the two of you were heading for reconciliation when I was there," Shayna said.

"We thought about it but realized we were just being drawn to what was familiar and comfortable for us. Arie knew that my heart was with you, and she cared enough to let go."

"How do you feel about her letting go again?"

"I appreciate her so much. Arie is my family. She's going to always be a part of my life. She knows me better than I know myself sometimes. I hope that you're OK with that."

"Yeah, I genuinely like Arie."

Greg lifted her chin, forcing her to look into his eyes.

"I'm glad to be back here with you."

"I must be madly in love with you. You're an unemployed photographer, and I still don't want to let go," she teased.

"I still have both studios. I'm far from being unemployed."

"Can I share something with you?" she asked.

"Of course," Greg answered.

"It's going to require us to leave the house. After we shower, I'll fix breakfast, and we can head out."

Greg raised both eyebrows at her.

"I like the sound of that." He groaned.

"Separate showers. We'll have plenty of time for that later," she said, tossing a pillow at him and jumping out of bed. Greg removed his shirt, following her to the shower. He was sure he had ways to make her change her mind.

CHAPTER 31

Shayna allowed the water to cascade down her body as she lathered her skin with Shea butter body wash. She closed her eyes as the steaming water stung her skin to her delight. The cool breeze that briefly passed caused her to shiver, and she knew Greg had entered the bathroom. She could feel him watching her as she applied soap to her body. He didn't say a word, and Shayna took the opportunity to give him a private show.

Shayna kept her eyes closed as her hands slid over her body, touching her small perky breasts, causing her nipples to harden. Her hands moved over her stomach before continuing their path downward and resting between her soapy thighs. She massaged the soap onto each long, shapely leg, bending over to give him a glimpse of her ass. She leaned her head back allowing the water to cover her head, springing her curls to life. She moaned as she stroked her now dripping wet hair. Her eyes opened and stared into Greg's lustful gaze. He was already naked and ready for her, and damn, was he a sight to behold. She smiled at him, encouraging him to join her.

Greg opened the shower door and stepped in. Shayna stepped backwards and allowed the water to spray him. She watched as the droplets raced down his chest. She followed the trail that led to his fullness and bit down on her lip, remembering the last time she'd had him. Their gaze met a second time, speaking only with their eyes. She was ready for him. This time, she wanted Greg more than she needed him. She allowed her hand to roam over his tattoo covered shoulder. She placed soap into her hands, using them to lather his body from head to toe. She allowed her hands to take the scenic route, stopping to linger on her favorite parts. He was giving her control if only for the moment, and Shayna took full advantage.

Once the soap was removed from his body, Shayna used her tongue to kiss away the water droplets from his lips. The innocent gesture turned into hunger as Greg lifted Shayna into the air. She wrapped her legs around his torso, forcing their bodies closer. He firmly pressed her against the wall as her hands frantically touched him. She could feel him growing even more between her parted legs as she gently sank her teeth into his neck. The moan he released encouraged Shayna to bite into his shoulder then his lips. She frantically devoured his soaking wet body as the water continued to spray his back.

"I need to hear you say you're ready, Shayna."

Shayna moaned as she nibbled his chin.

"Baby, tell me you're ready."

"Greg?"

"Yes?"

"Make love to me, baby. I'm ready," Shayna said, wrapping her arms around his neck. She peered into his eyes so he could see her sincerity.

Greg slid into her with ease. The moisture from the water made their union even sweeter. Shayna waited for him to touch that spot like he'd done the last time, but he didn't. He slid in and out of her slowly. The heat from the water and friction caused Shayna to lay her head back against the shower wall.

"Baby, please—"

"Shhh...I just want to take it slow with you this time. Let me enjoy you."

Greg was making her feel like a nympho, but his words soothed

145

her. His pumping motions caused her body to slide against the slippery shower walls, and she sank her nails into his back. He gripped her behind tightly so that he could feel every inch of her. Shayna allowed herself to enjoy the passion he put behind each movement. She placed a breast into his mouth, and he devoured it as he continued to make love to her. Shayna begged for more, and Greg gave her what she wanted with each thrust. The sound from the shower and their naked bodies meeting turned Shayna on even more. She felt so loved and wanted as he rested his face into her neck, their bodies pressed together heart to heart. Greg rammed into her hitting that spot. Shayna's orgasm was loud and throaty, and she didn't recognize her own voice.

"I love you, Greg," she moaned.

Those words caused Greg to release inside her, consummating their union.

GREG'S HEART pounded in his chest when Shayna finally pulled up to their destination. When she said she wanted to share something with him, he wouldn't have guessed this location. Once out of the car, Shayna wrapped her arms around his and ushered him closer, stopping only a few feet from where they parked.

"Greg, I'd like you to meet Shawn."

Greg looked down at the heart-shaped granite headstone with hand carved roses at the base. The stone read:

Shawn Wilson
10-11-87 to 03-31-13
Taken from our lives but never from our hearts.
XOXO

They stood in silence for what seemed like forever. Greg didn't know what to say, so he didn't. He felt that she was working through some things and just needed him there.

"This is what has kept me from openly loving you."

Shayna knelt down and used her hand to wipe away dirt that had settled on the headstone before taking a seat.

"It says it right there… 'taken from my life but never from my heart.' He's going to always have a piece of my heart. Last night, I was able to admit to myself that all of the rest is yours." Greg, still unable to speak, took a seat next to her and held her hand.

"Do you think you can love someone who's been so broken?" she asked.

"I'm already in love with someone who is perfect," Greg answered sincerely.

Shayna looked at him so lovingly that Greg pulled her close to him the top of her head.

"I'll give you a minute."

"No, don't leave. I want you here with me."

Greg grabbed her hand in his and held it to his heart. Shayna lay her head on his shoulder as they sat in silence, Shayna finally able to find comfort and closure.

CHAPTER 32

armen, Shayna, and Molina walked into the full movie theater. Molina headed to the concession stand while Shayna and Carmen picked up their preordered tickets from the kiosk.

"Hurry up, Molina! We are already late!" Carmen yelled.

"Good grief, Carmen. We're only a few minutes late. The credits haven't even started."

"You know the credits are my favorite part," Carmen countered.

"You just want to try to prove that you are smarter than we are with the lame trivia questions before the show."

"This is true, sister. You take the trivia questions way too serious," Shayna added.

"I do not. You guys are just saying that because you suck at it."

The trio walked into the theater, finding a seat in the middle row.

"I'm still shocked you wanted to see a movie of all things, Carmen. This is so not like you. What are we seeing anyway?" Shayna asked.

"Yeah, what are we seeing, Carmen?"

"First of all, Troy and TJ needed some bonding time without me, and I thought seeing a movie would be fun. The only thing out right now is *Superfly* and *Incredibles 2.*"

"So, we're watching *Incredibles 2?*" Molina teased.

"No, we're watching *Superfly*. Now, be quiet the movie is about to start."

They watched as the opening credits began, and in true Carmen fashion, she answered most of the trivia questions while throwing it in her sisters' faces. The lights dimmed, and four guys dressed in all denim appeared on the screen. They each had hoods over their heads, and their backs were turned. Music began to play, and the four guys did a smooth turn, so they were facing the camera. They wore sunglasses as they began lip singing "She's Playing Hard to Get" by Hi-Five. It took Shayna a moment to realize the men lip singing were Greg, Gavin, Drake, and Ryan. They were reenacting the music video with full choreography, wardrobe changes, and set designs as candid shots of Greg and Shayna popped up throughout the video. Some of the photos of her, Shayna had never seen. One was of her sleeping and a few others from the photoshoot she'd had with Carmen and Molina. Shayna felt the tears building as she realized what was happening. Molina and Carmen cheered and screamed along with the other movie goers as the guys sang *"she's playin' hard to get. She just won't admit. That she likes me. She likes me..."* while hitting every dance move to perfection. The audience laughed as Molina, playing the part of Shayna, disses Greg in one of the scenes. Shayna laughed and cried at the same time as the video came to an end with the guys doing impromptu dance moves on the set. The theater erupted with cheers and whistles as Greg came on the screen dressed in a black tuxedo, holding red roses. He looked amazing from what Shayna could see through her tears.

"Hey, baby. If I know you, you're probably crying right now. Carmen, give my baby a Kleenex."

Carmen did as she was instructed as a smiling Shayna dabbed at her eyes.

"When I met you, you told me you weren't easy. You were right about that, baby."

Carmen, Shayna, and Molina laughed out loud.

"Although the road has been bumpy, the reward has been more

than worth it. I want to spend the rest of my life getting to know you, Shayna King."

The video ended, and Molina and Carmen cooed while Shayna continued to dab at her eyes.

"Will you marry me, Shayna?"

The sisters turned around to see Greg on one knee in the middle of the aisle, holding out a ring box. Shayna covered her face and cried harder as her sisters consoled her, shedding tears of their own.

"Say yes! Say yes!" the audience chanted.

"I love you, sis, but you need to give the man an answer," Molina teased.

Shayna stood up and walked to Greg, who was still kneeling. It was then she noticed Drake, Ryan, Gavin, Q, Troy, and Arie standing behind him.

"Yes, I will spend the rest of my life with you," she said between sniffles.

Greg slid the ring on her finger before he stood and kissed her.

"Thank you for loving me the way you do," she whispered in his ear.

"I was made to love you."

Shayna lay her head on his shoulder as they embraced, and everyone cheered.

"Let's see the ring," Carmen said, grabbing Shayna's hand.

"Good job, brother," she said, admiring the princess cut, simple yet gorgeous diamond.

"Let me see," Molina said, joining them. "Congratulations, guys!"

Molina embraced Shayna and Greg.

"You guys rocked it out in the video. Seeing it put together was amazing!"

"I have to thank Arie for lending me her amazing crew. And of course, my amazing backup singers."

"Back up? I was the main attraction," Ryan said, causing laughter to erupt from the crowd.

"At least you guys made the cut," Troy added.

"Don't worry, baby. They just didn't want you to steal their shine," Carmen teased.

"Not true, but imagine this guy in 90's gear. It's just not him; he stood out like a sore thumb," Greg joked.

The group erupted in another round of laughter at the thought of Troy in the 90's throwback outfits they'd chosen.

"Yeah, I'm much better behind the camera."

"Gavin, I didn't know you had dance moves," Shayna added, catching him eyeing Molina, who was busy ignoring him. This was the first time they'd seen each other since Gavin discovered he had a child and ended their relationship. It was obvious he still loved her but felt he had to do what was best for his daughter.

"There's not much he can't do," Greg said.

"There's plenty I can't do," Gavin countered, still eyeing Molina.

"I have one question," Molina said, ignoring Gavin's gaze. "You all knew this was happening today, but no one thought to include me?"

"Because we all knew you would try to take over," Troy answered. Molina feigned shock.

"That is not true. Carmen is the perfectionist."

"Yes, but you are the most protective and would be all 'that's not good enough for my sister,'" Carmen mimicked.

"Touché. But only because I love my sisters, and you two deserve the best. I'm glad you've both found the best," she added.

"Let's get out of here and go celebrate! Arie has booked an amazing restaurant for the occasion. And with that being said, I would like to ask Arie if she would be my best woman? Without her wit, love, and support, I don't know if Shayna and I would be celebrating our union today."

"And the fact she fired you!" Ryan yelled, gaining more laughter.

"Yes, and the fact she fired me. Shayna, what do you think, baby?"

"I think it's an amazing idea."

"What do you say, Arie? Will you be my best woman?"

"I would love nothing more."

Shayna and Greg embraced her.

EPILOGUE

*S*hayna walked gracefully on the stretch of white sand as she made her way to her future husband. Greg stood under the flowered gazebo, looking as calm as the turquoise water that sparkled behind him. Not even the amazing view could dim Shayna's glowing light as she made eye contact with her beautiful sisters. They were marrying on the beach in Turks and Caicos after planning an amazing wedding in San Diego. Gavin, in an effort to win Molina back, asked if he could use Shayna and Greg's already planned wedding to marry Molina only a month earlier. It had been an amazing affair. Shayna was thrilled she'd been a part of Gavin and Molina's reunion, and because of their sacrifice, Gavin had gifted them an amazing destination wedding with all of their friends and family.

Molina stood with her new husband as Gavin held a smiling Chyna in his arms. Carmen stood next to Troy, who held on to a squirming TJ. Arie stood next to Greg as his best woman with tears in her eyes, and the sight caused Shayna to tear up. She'd been the reason Shayna and Greg's love story ended in happily ever after. Shayna was thrilled when Greg suggested she stand in as best woman.

Shayna's dress was simple and uncomplicated and complimented her figure nicely. She carried a bouquet of white lilies and placed one in her curls. Molina had passed down her mother's earrings, the same ones given to her by Carmen only a month earlier. Once she reached Greg, he reached out his hand to her, linking his fingers into hers.

"You look beautiful. I'm so lucky," he whispered for her ears only.

"Are we really getting married?"

"Yes, unless you're having second thoughts."

"Not on your life, Mr. Navarro," she said, beaming at him. They held hands as the minister began to speak.

"Dearly beloved, we are gathered here today in the sight of God to join this man and this woman in holy matrimony."

SHAYNA SAT front and center at their outside wedding reception as the guys repeated their Hi-Five routine. The guests cheered them on, laughing in the process. They'd included Troy as a fifth member, which made the routine ten times funnier. Shayna wiped away tears of laughter at the over dramatized dance movements the guys displayed. She looked up at Arie, who was standing next to her, whistling and cheering with the rest of the guests. Shayna reached out and grabbed her hand. Arie looked down at her quizzically, and Shayna mouthed the words *thank you*. Arie squeezed her hand.

"Promise me you'll be good to him."

"I promise."

The End

A NOTE FROM THE AUTHOR

I cannot thank you enough for all of the support you guys gave me on my first release! You guys sure know how to make a woman feel special. Thank you for taking a chance on a new author and sharing in this experience with me! I'm thrilled to bring you along on this new journey. I hope you fell in love with these characters as much as I did! I look forward to growing as a writer with your support. Stay tuned for book three of the King sisters' series. Troy and Carmen's love story is coming soon!

Love,

G. Fife

ABOUT THE AUTHOR

Gina Hayes-Fife of Louisville, Kentucky has been serving others for over twenty years in the customer service industry. The married mother of one has enjoyed reading and writing for as far back as she can remember.

Gina took a leap of faith and dove headfirst onto the literary scene in February 2018. She is a hopeless romantic, and as a result, plans to take the romance scene by storm. Gina is devoted to giving her readers classic love stories sure to melt their hearts.

When she isn't writing, Gina is a key member of the Autism community, helping to bring awareness and acceptance to those on the spectrum.

Stay connected

To keep up with future releases, characters, synopsis reveals, and sneak peeks, please subscribe to my website, authoressgfife.com

Join my book club, Red Carpet Romance, on Facebook to stay connected with me and other readers.

facebook.com/authoress.g.fife.5